"An engagemen[t]"

"That's only for roman[ce]
"And I'm not sure if this is okay. I feel like your parents want what is best for you. Are you sure Cassidy isn't? The best thing for you, I mean."

"I know she isn't," Joe said. "I'm not sure why she's here or what she or they think, but I've never been the person she wants."

"I see." She stepped into the stall and stood close to the mare. "I mean, I still need those Christmas decorations. And now, I need a lawyer for the twins' mother."

"Is this extortion?" He found it hard to be offended. She had that innocent look on her face but her silver-gray eyes sparkled with mirth.

"I mean, maybe." She laughed. "I consider it more of a trade. You need a fiancée. I need help."

"You're beautiful when you barter," he found himself saying. The words took them both by surprise. "And I'm rarely impulsive."

"Maybe you should be impulsive more often?"

He liked that idea. "Maybe so."

Maybe he should take her advice to heart…

Brenda Minton lives in the Ozarks with her husband, children, cats, dogs and strays. She is a pastor's wife, Sunday-school teacher, coffee addict and is sleep deprived. Not in that order. Her dream to be an author for Harlequin started somewhere in the pages of a romance novel about a young American woman stranded in a Spanish castle. Her dreams came true, and twenty-plus books later, she is an author hoping to inspire young girls to dream.

Books by Brenda Minton

Love Inspired

Mercy Ranch

Reunited with the Rancher
The Rancher's Christmas Match
Her Oklahoma Rancher
The Rancher's Holiday Hope
The Prodigal Cowboy
The Rancher's Holiday Arrangement

Bluebonnet Springs

Second Chance Rancher
The Rancher's Christmas Bride
The Rancher's Secret Child

Visit the Author Profile page at Harlequin.com for more titles.

The Rancher's Holiday Arrangement

Brenda Minton

LOVE INSPIRED
INSPIRATIONAL ROMANCE

LOVE INSPIRED®
INSPIRATIONAL ROMANCE

Recycling programs
for this product may
not exist in your area.

ISBN-13: 978-1-335-55397-3

The Rancher's Holiday Arrangement

Copyright © 2020 by Brenda Minton

This edition published by arrangement with Harlequin Books S.A.

For questions and comments about the quality of this book, please contact us at CustomerService@Harlequin.com.

Love Inspired
22 Adelaide St. West, 40th Floor
Toronto, Ontario M5H 4E3, Canada
www.Harlequin.com

Printed in U.S.A.

Not that I speak in respect of want:
for I have learned, in whatsoever state I am,
therewith to be content.
—*Philippians* 4:11

To Lori and Cari,
for being willing to read at the drop of a hat.

Chapter One

Mercy Ranch during the holidays sometimes overwhelmed Joe Lawson. He tended to be a solitary person. Not a loner, he just liked quiet and appreciated his own company. That said, he would never turn down an invitation to join Jack West, founder of the ranch for wounded veterans, his family or his housekeeper, Maria, who happened to be one of the best cooks in the state of Oklahoma.

Once dinner was over and everyone started socializing, Joe made his way out the door with the appropriate comments. *Thank you. See you later. Yes, that mare is about to foal.* No one asked where he was heading off to. They probably knew he needed to clear his head.

Sometimes a man just needed to be alone.

He headed for his truck, stopping to pet the brown standard poodle that followed him across the lawn as he headed for his truck that he'd left by the barn. If a person could call the building that housed offices, stalls and an indoor arena a barn.

"See you later, pup." He gave the dog a final pat on the head and climbed behind the wheel of his truck. He planned on driving west, about three miles to the other side of Hope. He'd noticed that a local ranch had come up for sale. The land was rolling hills, good stands of trees and a fairly new house.

He knew he'd come to a crossroads in his life. If he intended to stay in Oklahoma, he needed his own place. If he planned on going back to Connecticut, he needed to make a decision. Soon.

Unlike other pivotal moments in his life, this time he knew better than to be impulsive. He might have plans, but he also knew God in a way he hadn't before. Unlike his teens and twenties, Joe in his thirties was a praying man. A man of faith.

A mile outside of Hope, a truck pulled out from a paved county road, spinning gravel as it took off in front of him. Joe slowed to avoid hitting the other vehicle, then he kept his distance as the truck swerved from the shoulder to the opposite lane.

"Texting and driving," he muttered as he hit

his horn, hoping to get the attention of the other driver. The person needed a reminder that he wasn't alone on this stretch of road.

For a brief moment the truck straightened out and managed to stay between the lines. Joe relaxed until the truck jerked to the shoulder, hit the grass and then swerved across the center line as the driver made an overcorrection.

He watched, unable to do a thing as the truck swerved into the path of an oncoming vehicle, clipping the front and sending the small SUV careening off the road, down an incline.

The truck sped off. Joe pulled to the side of the road, grabbing his phone to call 911 as he jumped from his truck and hurried across the road and down the embankment. The sound of young children crying reached him, filling him with equal parts terror and relief. If they were crying, they had to be okay, right?

The dispatcher on the other end asked questions. Location. Types of vehicles involved. Specifics about the crash and victims. He gave what information he could, but he was impatient to get to the people in that SUV.

"A blue truck, mid-eighties model and with obvious damage to the front driver's side. Hit and run. I don't know how many people in the vehicle, but I know there are children." He ended the call and hurried down the side of the hill, saying a prayer as he went.

As a volunteer for the local fire department, he'd worked more than his share of accidents. He knew he'd never get used to this, hurrying toward a wreckage, hearing children crying, hearing the frantic voice of a parent. But voices were preferable to silence. That much he knew.

The vehicle had rolled, but it had come to rest wheels down.

As he drew near the wreckage, a woman's voice rose above the cries that he now realized were babies. Babies with frantic, plaintive cries.

"We're going to be okay. Shhh, it's going to be okay."

Joe could hear the thread of panic in her voice, but their cries diminished somewhat as they listened to her soothing voice. He hurried to the driver's side of the vehicle, which appeared to have taken the brunt of the accident. The top and side were pushed in. The driver was pushing at her door, trying to get out.

"Hold on. I'm going to help you," he yelled as he rounded the vehicle to the passenger side. No way would the driver's side door open.

The passenger side wasn't much better. He moved to the back.

"Hey in there. I'm going to try to find a way

to get you out," Joe assured her as he looked for the latch on the back hatch. "Are you all okay?"

"We're okay." Her voice sounded weak. "We need to get out of here."

"I'm working on it."

The babies were crying again. She sounded as if she might be about to cry herself. Joe's insides tensed. He had to get them out of the vehicle. Now.

"Unlock the doors and I'll see if I can pull the back hatch open."

He heard the click and he pulled on the hatch, wishing he had two good arms and maybe a crowbar. He didn't have either. He had one good arm and a mighty God. With a whispered prayer he gave the hatch another hard pull. The door creaked open. He reached under and pushed it the rest of the way up, giving him room to crawl into the back, amid the jumble of chaotic luggage, to the sound of crying babies and the woman trying to comfort them as she worked to get out of her seat and crawl through the back.

Crawling, he made it to the middle row of seats where the babies were strapped in to car seats, upset but seemingly uninjured. He did a double take, looking at the redheaded, blue-eyed little girls. Twins. And from the looks of them, identical.

"Well now, aren't you a couple of cuties," he

interjected mid-chorus. Big tears rolled down round cheeks as blue eyes overflowed.

The driver had climbed through and placed herself in front of the car seat on his left. Joe's gaze collided with silver-gray eyes. Those molten gray eyes could only belong to one person, with a tangle of dark hair framing a face he remembered well.

Shocked at seeing her, he moved a little too quickly and the SUV rocked. She steadied herself as she worked to unlatch the restraints on the car seat.

"How can I help?" he asked as he straddled suitcases and remained still to keep the SUV from rocking again.

"Don't move?" she suggested, her focus on the baby she was freeing from the seat.

"There you go, sweetie. You're safe. I've got you." She spoke softly, her voice calmer than he would have expected. She glanced back again, and this time she recognized him. Briefly, she closed her eyes and a sigh slipped from her lips. "You."

"Me," he agreed.

"Of course," she muttered.

"Better me than no one at all," he told her.

"I won't argue." She held the baby close as she moved to the right. "Can you take her?"

"Yes, I can take her." He reached out with his left arm. "Daisy, you have to hand her to me."

Jack West's long-lost daughter shot him another look as she handed one baby to him. He took the little girl, smiling into blue eyes and adjusting so that he could take her with his left hand and transfer her to the right arm where he held her tight against his shoulder.

"Now get her sister and hand her to me so you can climb back here. I hear sirens. It won't be long till we have help." He kept his voice low, hoping to soothe the baby he held.

"Can you do this?" Daisy asked. "I mean…"

What she meant was, with his right arm amputated from the elbow down, could he manage the redheaded twins that were crying for their mama and struggling to be anywhere other than in the arms of a stranger.

"I know what you mean. Let's just get this done."

"Okay. Let me get Miriam." Daisy focused her attention on the second baby.

The little girl he held wrapped her arms around his neck. She was a tiny bundle of tears, strong arms and heartache, and at that moment he would have given the little one anything he owned to make her happy again.

Her tears were soaking his shirt and her sobs shook her little body. He began to sing a hymn from church, rocking just slightly to calm her. As he sang, both girls quieted.

"Keep singing," Daisy whispered. "Please keep singing."

Hearing the panic in her voice, he nodded, continuing to sing "Jesus Loves Me." The little redhead in his arms now rested against him. He soothed her, rubbing her back with his left hand.

Daisy faltered a little as she pulled the second baby from her seat. She leaned against the seat and breathed deeply, her eyes closed as she whispered words of comfort, promising everything would be okay.

"Are you able to get out?" Joe asked. "You can hand her to me."

"I'm good." She had the baby in her arms. "I can probably climb through with her."

"Slow and steady. You landed in a dry creek bed and the ground is uneven so your vehicle isn't going to be steady."

"I've got this," she told him.

"I know you do, but I can help you." The words were familiar, similar to words spoken at another time, in another place. Their gazes connected and her silver-gray eyes slid closed for just a moment, giving away the fact that she remembered their last encounter.

He reached for her, taking hold of her right arm to help her navigate the space between the seats as she climbed through to the back, pausing when the vehicle wobbled. He kept her close to his side, and they waited a long minute before edging toward the opening that would see them safely out of the SUV.

"We're almost there."

She didn't reply. Not to him. Her face was buried in the red curls of the baby that clung to her. She spoke softly, repeatedly telling the child she was safe. They were safe.

Joe eased through the narrow opening of the hatch, pausing as the vehicle rocked back and forth. He moved to the side and Daisy exited with the child she still held close. They were all safe. Joe took a deep breath, thanking his Maker for small victories. Next to him, Daisy shivered. He became aware of the chill of the autumn air.

"We need to get you up this hill," Joe told her. "The three of you need to get warm."

"The girls' coats are somewhere in my car," Daisy told him. "I should get their coats."

"They're probably full of shattered glass. We'll get you up the hill and into a warm car. Come on."

Sirens pierced the air and emergency vehicles arrived, lining the shoulder of the road. Joe, Daisy and the twins topped the hill as the first of the fire trucks and emergency vehicles arrived. Next to him, Daisy shivered and hugged the baby she held closer. Joe moved to her other side, hoping to shelter them from the wind that had picked up.

"Anyone else in there?" Derrick, an EMT that Joe had worked other accidents with, called out as he headed their way.

"No one else," Joe answered as he shifted the baby he carried. Her arms tightened around his neck, and she cried for her mama.

Daisy turned. Her eyes flickered with pain, but she managed a smile for the little girl in his arms. "We're okay, Myra. Everything is okay, sweetie."

He noticed then that she had a gash at her hairline above her ear. Daisy seemed to notice, as well. She touched the spot and winced.

"Don't look at me like that. I'm just fine. I know my name, the day of the week and where I am."

"I'm sure you're fine," Joe assured her. "It's just a cut."

"Would you like me to take one of the little ones from you?" Derrick asked.

"Maybe you could help Daisy," Joe suggested.

Derrick reached for the little girl Daisy held. At first the baby refused, burying her face against the woman she called Mama. Derrick kept talking, the way a man talked if he knew a thing or two about kids. Eventually the little girl turned and held her arms out to him.

"What's her name?" Derrick asked as he held the little girl close.

"Miriam," Daisy said, her teeth chattering.

"We should get them inside where they can warm up and we can clean that cut," Derrick said, already heading toward the faded red rescue vehicle.

Joe nodded in the direction of the rescue vehicle. She gave him a look that hovered between pain, distrust and obstinance. It wasn't the first time she'd given him that look. Several years back he'd come upon her in another situation that she'd needed help extricating herself from. He doubted she wanted to be reminded of that memory.

"Joe, I need to get a statement," a county deputy said as he headed their way.

"It can wait," Joe told him. "At least let us get them warmed up and calmed down."

He kept Daisy moving in the direction of help and let the deputy follow. Derrick was climbing out of the back of the old ambulance, blankets in hand.

"Where is Miriam?" Daisy asked, panic lacing her tone.

"She's fine," Derrick assured her. "She's with Talia, our other first responder. Tally is getting her wrapped up in a blanket. If you want to hand over that little girl, we'll get her checked out and warmed up."

Derrick started to wrap a blanket around Daisy's shoulders. She moved away from the first responder, her eyes going a little wild. Joe knew that look. He knew it had nothing to do with the moment or Derrick. In that moment, Daisy West was somewhere else, another time, another situation.

He knew from experience how a moment could suddenly drag a person into the past and how memories could become nightmares. Her fingers tangled in the scarf she wore around her neck and her eyes darted up, catching his.

"Let me help you, Daisy," he said softly. "We need to get you all warmed up and take a look at the cut."

He handed Myra to Derrick. The little girl whimpered but the first responder started to sing, rocking her as he headed inside the vehicle with her. Joe turned his attention to the woman at his side.

"Daisy?" He reached for the gauze and antiseptic Derrick had left on the back of the vehicle.

She nodded, and a tear leaking from one silver-gray eye slid down her cheek.

He brushed hair back from the side of her face. "Close your eyes."

She did and he pushed the gauze against the gash. She jerked away from him. For a moment her eyes went a little wild, causing him to pull back.

The scarf around her neck had come loose.

Color drained from her face and she swayed a bit.

"Daisy?"

"I'm fine." She started to take a step away from him. "I just…" She blinked a few times and wavered on her feet.

Daisy's legs buckled and Joe managed to get behind her in time to keep her from falling. He scooped her up in his arms and carried her to his truck.

Daisy pulled herself back to consciousness as Joe dumped her rather unceremoniously in the back seat of his truck. As she blinked away the fog, he was there, his face close to hers. His eyes, the hazel browns and greens of the forest, reflected his concern. She instantly wanted him to care and then just as quickly knew the heartache that came from trusting a look, a softly spoken word, from a man.

"Are you with me?" he asked.

"I'm fine. I need to get the twins. They're already frightened. I need to be with them."

"We'll get the twins, but I'm calling Carson and we're going to meet him at his office."

"You can't tell me what to do," she muttered. But he could, she realized. She might argue but she knew when to give in. This was one of those moments. Her head was pounding. She obviously needed to see a doctor. Even if the doctor was her older brother.

Joe ignored her weak attempt at arguing and motioned the deputy forward. The officer had both twins, one in each arm. Joe reached for Myra first, tucking her in next to Daisy and then he turned and reached for Miriam. Daisy situated a twin on either side and buckled them both in. She put an arm around each and held them close, comforted by their nearness. She'd gotten so used to having them close. Funny how life changed in a matter of months. What had started as a temporary inconvenience had become her new normal. Her heart was invested in the twins.

"We need our car seats," she objected as Joe leaned in to look at them. "This isn't safe."

He ignored her. That felt safer than his overprotectiveness with the quiet voice that was meant to soothe.

"No car seat, sorry. They're full of glass. It's

only a mile drive to Carson's office. I'll drive safely."

She glanced out the window at the SUV being sprayed with foamy water from the fire truck. "I was driving safely when this happened."

"I know you were." Again, those forest green-brown eyes of his, filled with compassion. Again with the quiet, "you're close to the edge" voice. "I'll have Dan give us an escort. Lights on. No one will speed around us or past us."

She wanted to agree with his plan, but she couldn't. A sob welled up and she buried her face in her hand, breathing through it because she wasn't going to cry. Not yet. Not until she was alone.

Joe glanced away and she silently thanked him for the moment of privacy. It didn't last. The deputy returned to his side.

"Miss West, I'm sorry to bother you, but I need to ask you a few questions."

Joe stepped between them, "Not right now, Dan."

"Joe, I have to write a report."

"I know you do. And I have to get these three to the doctor. They're freezing cold. Miss West has a gash that probably needs stitches. You can stop by later and ask all the questions you want."

Dan, the deputy, shook his head. "You aren't making this easy."

"No, I'm not." Joe grinned at the deputy. "And while you're at it, if you could give us an escort? Nothing like a parade when you come home, right, Daisy?"

Daisy frowned at him, happy to have him shifting the mood. "It's what I always dreamed of."

What she hadn't dreamed of was coming home and, for a second time, being rescued by Joe Lawson. The first time had been several years ago, the day of her father's open-heart surgery.

She'd fallen apart that night and Joe had been the person who found her.

If he mentioned it, she didn't know what she'd say. Would she tell him the truth, that her memories of that night were vague? What she remembered still brought a rush of heat to her face.

"I need to get it now, Joe." The officer stood a little taller, as if he thought to intimidate Joe Lawson.

"You and I both know you can wait until after she's been checked, Dan," Joe said with a deep voice of authority. He was several inches over six feet, broad across the shoulders and not the most handsome man Daisy had ever seen. But she thought he was about the most masculine. "I probably saw more than she did. The truck crossed the center line, overcorrected and hit the shoulder on the west bound lane and then overcorrected again. I'm assuming he was probably texting and driving. She didn't have time to brake. He clipped her front end, as you can see from her damaged car. She went into the ditch and overturned."

"We've put out information on the truck," Dan told him. "I'll give you that escort to Dr. West's."

Joe closed the door. A moment later he was behind the wheel and they were heading toward Hope. That's when the questions would start, and she needed to be ready with answers. There would be questions about more than her medical condition. Carson would want to know why she was in Hope, why on Thanksgiving and he would want to know about the twins.

"You could just take me to my place," she told the cowboy charmer who hadn't said a word since he got in the truck.

Her teeth chattered as she spoke, and she clenched her jaw to keep him from hearing. He cranked up the heat, then handed her the jacket thrown over the seatback. She took it and smoothed it over them, noticing that it smelled of horses, hay and aftershave.

"Your place?" He glanced her way, just briefly. "You mean Mercy Ranch?"

She sighed because she didn't want to tell him why she was here. Not that people wouldn't find out. It was a small town, under two thousand people. The kind of place where everyone knew everything about everyone else. She might as well get it over with.

"I have a house."

"In Hope?"

"Yes, in Hope. You can take me there." The coat and the heater weren't helping. She felt as if the cold had seeped into her bones and she couldn't get warm.

"I'm not taking you anywhere other than Carson's office. I texted him before we left, and he's waiting for you. Funny, he didn't know you were in town."

"It really isn't any of his business. Or yours, for that matter." Her jaw hurt from trying to calm the chattering.

"You're right about that. None of my business," he responded in an Oklahoma drawl that didn't sound quite right with the remains of his East Coast accent. He glanced back and she saw concern in his eyes.

"Then take me to 110 Prairie Rose."

His eyebrow arched. "Really? The old Macomb place?"

"Yes, it's the Daisy West place now. I bought it a couple months ago."

"Hmm," was his response. Then he was pulling into the gravel parking lot of her brother's medical office. He parked near the front door and before he could get out, Carson exited the building.

Her brother's presence brought a myriad of emotions, none particularly pleasant. Even the relief at seeing him wasn't exactly pleasant. She'd held on to anger and resentment like a cranky Chihuahua. That's what her friend Becky Stanford had told her. Becky's memory brought tears that Daisy quickly blinked away. Her friend's passing had brought Daisy back home, where she felt a need to be, back in the lives of her brothers and their new families. Back in her father's life.

None of it came easy. Her father would be the most difficult one to come to terms with.

She had to deal with the past, with all her anger and resentment.

Carson opened the back door of the truck and gave her that brotherly, concerned, doctor look of his. It didn't help. He hadn't been there when she'd needed him most. He'd gone to medical school, gotten married, left. He hadn't been there.

Not that his life had been a bed of roses. They'd all suffered at the hands of their parents. Carson had suffered through the loss of his wife. As a family, they had grieved.

"Welcome home, Daisy Jane." Carson reached for her but she didn't go to his arms. She handed him Myra, using the little girl as a buffer for the emotions she didn't want to deal with. She scooped Miriam up and exited the truck.

"Let's get you all inside and warmed up." Carson turned her toward the building. "I'm glad Joe brought you here."

"He wouldn't take no for an answer," she murmured.

"No?" Carson glanced back at her as he pushed the door open. "Count yourself blessed, because if you need someone in a crisis, he's probably the best."

"It shouldn't have happened."

"Accidents happen. That's why they're called 'accidents,' Daisy." Carson helped her inside his office. "You're pretty banged up. But the twins appear to be fine."

"They were snug in their seats and napping. It was a horrible way for them to wake up. I just wanted to go home and get them settled."

"Home?" Carson helped her onto the exam table, then placed Myra on her lap. He gave her a steady look in the eyes, flashing a small light at her pupils. "To Tulsa?"

She glanced at the cowboy in the doorway,

holding Miriam in his arms as she messed with the brim of his cowboy hat. He watched Daisy, as if waiting to see how she'd answer. As if he expected her to lie.

She turned her attention back to her brother. "It's Thursday, November 26. It's cold for this time of year. I don't have a head injury." She made eye contact with the cowboy. "I live at 110 Prairie Rose, in Hope. Surprise."

"Definitely a surprise." Carson opened a cabinet and pulled out a blanket that he wrapped around her shoulders and Myra. "Let's get you up on the table so I can examine you. And I'll trade you blankets. This one is warm."

She took the blanket, thankful for its warmth and wrapped it around herself and Myra. Carson retrieved another and wrapped it around Joe and Miriam.

"This isn't the way I planned my entrance into town. This isn't how I planned on telling you all."

"Isn't it?"

She managed a smile, but it hurt to make the gesture. She wiggled her jaw and it seemed fine, merely bruised. "I was working up the courage," she admitted. "And maybe trying to figure out for myself what I'm doing here."

Joe had left, taking Miriam with him. She

knew the little girl would be fine in his care. Yet she still felt a hint of panic.

"Breathe deep and slowly exhale," Carson told her.

"I'm fine."

"Of course you are. You've always said you're fine, even when you aren't. Can I look at your arm?"

"Of course." She held it out for him and he examined it, his expression thoughtful.

"It's sprained. I can arrange for X-rays but I don't think it's necessary." He touched her face, her jaw, the gash on her brow. "This is going to require stitches. But it won't leave much of a scar."

The word scar set them both on edge. He backed up, his smile disappearing. She sat there remembering stitches that *had* left a scar. Funny how just one word could steal her breath, cause her to relive the night her ex-husband had left her bleeding on the floor, payback for calling the police. She wanted to say it had been the worst night of her life, but thanks to her father and her stepfather, there were several worst nights.

None as bad as that night, though.

Her husband had been her first love, the one who was meant to replace all the other bad memories. He'd been overprotective, sheltering her, always wanting to know where she was and when she'd be home. She'd been too young to realize what all those traits hid. Until it had been too late.

As Carson gently cleaned the wounds on her face, Joe reappeared in the doorway, Miriam hugging his neck tight. "Got any cookies around this place?" he asked Carson.

"In a container in the fridge and there is juice, too. Kitchen is at the end of the hall on the right." Carson glanced back, smiling at the sight of the big cowboy and the tiny redhead clinging to him. "Got yourself a new friend?"

"I'm not a kid person," he insisted.

"Looks like you are," Carson countered. "If you get those two, I'll get the snack and meet you in the waiting room."

Joe moved Miriam to his right arm and the little girl obliged by wrapping her arms around his neck. Carson took Myra from Daisy and handed her over to the cowboy. She went without complaint, cuddling in to him. He gave Daisy a questioning look before he left the room.

Her brother also left, and for a moment Daisy was alone. She pulled the blanket tight and closed her eyes, needing a minute to pull herself together.

"You okay?" Carson asked a moment later.

She opened her eyes, nodding as she lifted her face to meet his curious gaze. "I'm good."

"It would be okay if you weren't," he countered.

"Could we just get this over with?" Daisy flinched as her brother picked up a syringe. "Yes, we can. This is going to sting."

He was wrong; it more than stung. Her eyes shot open. "Hey!"

"Sorry." Carson leaned in close. "Just a few stitches and you'll be good as new."

"Of course I will."

"Maybe not tonight. Or even tomorrow. Soon." He leaned in closer, working quickly. She cringed at each tug.

"All done," he said after a couple of minutes, which seemed longer. "I don't want you to be alone tonight."

"I'll have the girls with me. I'm not alone."

He stepped back, found his stool and moved it to sit in front of her. "Daisy, just this once, please trust me. You can't be alone tonight. I'm going to keep you awake, feed you and probably shove medicine into you. Come on, you love Kylie. You love your niece and nephew. Kylie is going to want to smother you and these little girls with attention."

Joe reappeared at the door. The girls each had a bag of cookies. His hat was tipped at an awkward angle, as if it had been jolted from his head.

"Let me check the girls now," Carson said. He motioned Joe into the exam room, all six-foot-whatever of him. A mountainous man with dark hair, a lopsided cowboy hat and a grin that changed him from plain to…more.

She took the girls from him, feeling safer, more secure with them on her lap. They were hers, at least for the time being, until their mother could care for them again. They had changed her life, made her rethink her dreams, her future. They'd allowed her to let go of the chain of clothing stores she'd built from nothing. Then she'd invested the money from the sale in a one-hundred-year-old house with good bones, as her contractor had told her upon inspection.

The twins began to fuss.

"I'm going to head back to the ranch. Unless you need me." Joe pulled a couple of packages of cookies out of his pocket and handed them to her. "They might want these."

"Thank you," she said, taking the cookies. "For everything."

"I'll stop by and check on you tomorrow."

Ugh, he was thoughtful. Those were the most dangerous types of men. They snuck in with their kind gestures, their considerate actions, then in an instant they left a woman scarred for life.

Chapter Two

Joe drove through town the next morning doing a decent job of keeping his mind on the mare back at the ranch, the one about to foal, plus the property he planned on viewing at the beginning of the week. He most definitely was not thinking about Daisy West or about the twins, Myra and Miriam.

Except that he *was* thinking about them. He'd spent more time than he liked to admit thinking about Daisy West. It had started a few years back when he'd come upon her in a bad situation. He'd thought about her. Prayed for her. Avoided her. Even when he'd seen her at her brothers' weddings, he'd managed to keep his distance. And she'd kept hers.

If she was going to be living in Hope, he guessed avoiding her would no longer be an option. The question he ought to ask himself was, why did he feel the need to avoid her?

That was a question for another day.

As he drove past Zac Akins's garage, Zac flagged him down. Up until that moment, he'd been doing a pretty decent job of minding his own business. The frantic waving meant he couldn't drive on past. He pulled in next to the garage and got out of his truck.

"What's up?" Joe asked the garage owner, a man about his age and a former resident of Mercy Ranch.

Zac had been a mechanic in the army. He'd joined the residents of Mercy Ranch after healing from third degree burns. When the old gas station had come up for sale, Zac had bought it, added a garage and a tow service.

"I have Jack's daughter's SUV. No one has been by to get Daisy's stuff. I brought it all inside. Would you mind taking it out to the ranch?"

"I don't think she's staying at the ranch. Do you want me to give Carson a call and have him come by?" Because the last thing Joe wanted to do was get more involved than he already was.

The man looked perplexed. "Yeah, I suppose Carson could come by."

Zac glanced in the direction of his office, and Joe realized the problem. Through the windows, he could see that the place was jam-packed with Daisy's suitcases and the two car seats.

"I vacuumed the car seats and made sure all of the glass from that window was off everything." Zac shrugged. "I hope she and those little girls are okay. I heard they got the young man that hit them."

"I'm glad they got him. People don't think about how quickly an accident can happen." Joe took a step back, thinking how easy he could shrug this off and leave it for one of the West brothers to deal with. It was a good plan. Until it wasn't. Until he was heading for the office. "I'll load this stuff up and take it to her. I know you need your office back."

"I'd sure appreciate that, Joe. I'll help you get it loaded."

That's how Joe ended up with suitcases, infant car seats and a purse in his possession. It was also how he ended up on the narrow street that led to Daisy West's new house. A phone call to Carson had led him this way after learning that Daisy had insisted on being dropped off at her house early that morning. Against her brother's wishes, of course.

He pulled around the circle drive and stopped in front of the brick-sided, two-story Georgian structure. He'd seen the house before. It sat on the end of a dead-end street, a barn and five acres making it an ideal place for someone wanting to be in town but still have space.

As Joe headed up the sidewalk, his second trip, carrying the rest of her suitcases, the front door opened. Daisy, tall and slim with her dark hair in a ponytail and a vibrant scarf around her neck, stared at him. She definitely didn't seem thrilled to see him.

He let it go and shifted his attention to the identical little girls, Myra and Miriam, that she held in her arms. He didn't know their ages, but he would guess under a year.

"How are you feeling this morning?" he asked as he stood there surrounded by her luggage. The twin on her right hip grinned and reached for him, her bright blue eyes sparkling with mischief. "Myra or Miriam?"

"Myra," Daisy answered, shadows beneath her eyes. "Miriam is not quite as outgoing. She's actually very clingy, as you can see."

Miriam was practically glued to Daisy and kept her face hidden in the floral scarf Daisy wore.

"Whose children are they?" he asked as he stood there on the porch, making faces at the child in his arms. The little girl tugged on his hat, and he took it off and settled it on her head. The little girl giggled when it dropped down over her eyes. He pulled it up and peeked at her, making her giggle again. "We have to get you a hat of your own."

He settled the hat back on his own head and turned his attention back to Daisy, realizing when he did, she had a way of catching him off guard.

"I'm a foster parent," she answered. "Why are you here?"

He pointed at the obvious pile of her belongings. "I have your suitcases and car seats. Zac at the garage towed your car in yesterday. He cleaned this all up for you. No glass."

"That's kind of him. And you, of course. But I could have gotten it."

"I know you could have, but I was driving by and Zac needed his office back. You don't travel light."

She laughed, and the action seemed to take her by surprise. "I have never traveled light and I've learned that with twins, I will never travel light. They require a lot of stuff. You should see what all has to be moved next week. I'll be unpacking for a year."

"We'll have a housewarming party and invite everyone to help," he suggested.

"I don't think so."

"Let me carry this hat-stealing cowgirl back in for you and I'll get your stuff."

"Thank you." She paused. "I appreciate that.

They're heavy, and with both of them wanting to be held, I don't get a lot done."

He didn't want to wade into this family situation, but the words were out before he could stop them. "You have a family that is more than willing to help you out. I can guarantee, they've dragged me out of the bottom of a pit that I didn't think I'd ever climb out of."

"Is this the part where you tell me how my father put you back on track and fixed you?" she asked sharply.

"Nah, I don't think so. My journey and my relationship with your father are mine. You'll have to figure out your own and work on that the best way you know how."

She bit down on her bottom lip, studying his face, not lowering her gaze to his arm.

"The only advice I'll give you, Daisy West, is be willing to accept help." Then he slipped past her, entering the foyer with Myra clinging to his neck. "Where to?"

"There's a playpen in the sitting room." She pointed to the door on the right. He headed that way with the little girl that had gone from playing with his hat to rubbing sleep-filled eyes. He didn't know much about kids, but he knew that babies drank from a bottle. He placed her in the pen and handed her a bottle that was on the table. She took it with a sleepy smile and shoved it in her mouth, curling on her side and reaching for a stuffed animal. He watched for a moment, just to make sure she was sleeping.

Daisy stood nearby, Miriam in her arms, a soft expression on her face that quickly disappeared when he glanced her way.

"I'll get your luggage," he told her as he slipped out the door.

She followed, and as they stepped onto the front porch, a car was turning off the street. It pulled behind his truck and stopped. Joe knew the car. From the look on Daisy's face, so did she.

Jack West, Daisy's father, sat in the passenger seat. His longtime housekeeper, Maria, was behind the wheel.

"Did you tell him?" Daisy asked. Or rather, she accused him.

"Nope. Not my business," he assured her as he grabbed a suitcase and carried it inside the wide, two-story-high foyer.

"Carson must have told him," she said. "This is what I get for coming back here. Everyone wants to be involved in my life and in my business."

"That's called family. If you didn't want it, why come back?" He grabbed another suitcase.

"Says the guy who's thousands of miles away from his family." She said it with a knowing expression that he found kind of cute. It was a saucy look, as if she'd one-upped him.

In that look he saw the Daisy West he'd like to know better. He wanted to get married someday. He wanted a wife and kids. The problem was, this woman didn't know herself. Or God.

That put her firmly off-limits.

"I should go over there." She started to take a step but then stopped. "This is harder than I thought it would be."

"You know that he's getting older, and his health…"

"I do understand that." She closed her eyes briefly. When she opened them, she looked at him. "I'm not sure why you keep turning up in my life like this."

"Pardon?"

She pinned him with a look. "The worst times. Tulsa, after my dad's surgery. Yesterday, with the accident. Today."

"It isn't as if I've made a habit of rescuing you," he told her. "Two times, I happened to be at the right place at the right time, and I'm not sorry. Now hand over that baby and go greet your father."

"Why are you so nice to me?" she asked, seeming as if she really wanted an answer. As if there was an answer other than just human kindness.

"Guess it's just who I am?" He took the baby from Daisy and stepped back into her house, turning to face her. He winked, hoping to lighten the mood. "You're okay, Daisy. Just say hello and see where it takes you."

"I don't remember what happened that night," she whispered to him as she walked away, closing the door behind her.

He felt his heart pound wildly inside his rib cage. He wanted to call her back, to ask her what she thought had happened that night he'd given her a ride home. Had she lived with memories that weren't real, were only imagined? He'd left his number for her to call, and she never had.

It had been three years. He hadn't given it a lot of thought. He considered what he did a good deed. He'd helped the daughter of a man who had given him a second chance at life.

Maybe he should have called her?

Daisy left Joe standing in her foyer holding Miriam. She walked out the front door, closing it behind her, then leaned against the heavy wood barricade, needing the solid strength between them. She drew in a deep breath and told herself to be calm. After all, this was why she'd come back to her hometown. She had come to Hope, knowing it was time to make things right.

She wanted her brothers, their families and even Jack in her life.

So she stood there as Jack and Maria made their way to her front porch. Jack leaned heavily on his walker, tears streaming down his weathered cheeks. Maria remained at his side, a hand on his back, her own eyes overflowing. Daisy was determined not to cry.

"Jack," she spoke firmly. She hadn't called him Dad since her mother took her and her brothers all of those years ago. They'd left in the middle of the night and never looked back. "I guess I'm not surprised Carson told you where to find me."

"That's my girl. Never Back Down Daisy." Jack's voice trembled, but the light in his eyes and the smile were both strong. "Mind if I come in and sit a spell?"

"Please come in." She tried not to think about the nickname. She'd somehow managed to forget that he'd called her that as a child.

Never Back Down Daisy. She'd been his spitfire. She'd been strong and determined, stubborn, even as a child. He used to tell a story of how she'd walked herself into the barn as a toddler and entered the stall of his stallion. He'd found her there, arms around the animal's legs and the horse had been shaking, scared to death of the tiny person in his domain.

She hadn't felt brave in years. What she had now was an illusion of bravery. She was every old building in this town of his, decorated on the outside to hide all the broken bits inside. It didn't matter how much he painted and repaired, this was still an old town, forgotten by time and tourists who had moved on to bigger and brighter attractions.

She was just as broken. As if to remind herself, she touched the scarf at her neck, keeping it in place to hide the scars.

She was broken, except for one very important piece to this puzzle. She no longer wanted to be the broken person she'd become. She didn't want to fix up the exterior with a smile and a show of bravery. She wanted to actually be brave. She wanted to be the Daisy of old, the little girl who would take a horse by the legs and not fear. She wanted to make peace with her past.

She'd started the process with her mother, now divorced from Martin, the man who had taken up the abuse of her children after she'd left Jack.

Jack was the last mountain to tackle. He was her Everest. Jack was the real reason she'd come home, to Hope.

She led her father and Maria through the foyer to the front sitting room where Jack stopped upon seeing his ranch foreman sprawled on the floor, playing with the twins. Joe sat up, straightening the black cowboy hat Myra had pushed down on her own head, bending it a bit. He didn't scold her for that crease in the brim of a hat Daisy knew hadn't come cheaply.

"I should go," Joe said as he took the hat from the little girl and pushed it back on his head, where it belonged.

"Not on my account," Jack said with a funny grin. "I kind of like seeing you down there with those baby girls. Now, aren't they pretty little things. Daisy, where'd you get those little girls?"

"The gettin' place," Daisy quipped.

Her dad laughed as she'd known he would. Some things didn't change.

But he had. He'd changed and become someone different, someone respected, beloved, looked up to. He'd been invited to Washington, DC, but he'd refused. He'd been written up in magazines, honored by the military.

Why did all of that, things that should have made her proud, make her angrier? Because he was that person to so many people, but she didn't know him as anything other than the man who had been drunk and angry throughout her childhood?

"Daisy?" Joe's voice sifted through the chaotic thoughts and images, dragging her back to the present and to her father's question.

"They're my foster daughters," she explained. "Their mother worked for me at my main store. She made some mistakes in her life."

"I won't judge anyone for making mistakes. I'm well aware of how they sneak up on a person." Jack sat down, sighing as he went. "You've already furnished the place, and we weren't even aware you'd bought it."

She glanced around the room with the pale gray walls, turquoise blue furnishings and no family pictures anywhere.

"Surprise," she said as she scooped up Miriam. The twins had altered her life. Even if— or when—they went back to their mother, she knew her life would forever be changed. Joe moved, drawing her attention as he pushed to his feet, holding Myra in his left arm.

Joe knew the meaning of life altering. He had lived through a catastrophic injury while serving in Afghanistan, and he had made a life for himself at Mercy Ranch.

"It's a nice surprise," Maria said, "having you here. We wish you could have joined us for Thanksgiving."

"Family holidays are a bit much for me," Daisy said, smiling to soften the words. Maria was kind and didn't deserve her anger.

"I have choir practice. If you need any-thing…" Joe glanced at his watch, clearly un-comfortable with her little family reunion.

"Thank you, I'm good." She smiled, letting him go. And then, before she could stop her-self and for no reason whatsoever, she placed Miriam in the playpen where he'd put Myra and followed him. "I'll walk you out."

In the foyer he stood near the door, his hat tilted back just enough that she had a clear view of his eyes. Eyes that reminded her of a forest. Moss, trees and earth. He grinned at her, turn-ing her insides to mush.

"Are you using me as a way to escape your father? I wouldn't have guessed you to be a chicken, Daisy West."

"I'm not a chicken, Joe Lawson. I'm polite. You came to check on me. You brought my lug-gage over. The very least I can do is walk you to the door."

"Oh, so this is about manners, is it?" He winked at her.

"Stop flirting."

"I'm not flirting," he said, letting his smile drift away. "I'm being charming. I'm not very good at it, so it probably comes off as either awkward or flirting."

"Well, stop. I don't like it." She didn't want

him to flirt. She didn't want him to be a friend or to be someone who could hurt her.

"I will try my best not to be charming," he assured her as his hand went to the doorknob. "Are you going to be okay? If you need me to stay, I can."

"There's no need," she informed him. "I think you've rescued me enough this week. Maybe someday I can return the favor."

"We…we need to talk about the night I took you home."

The words chased away the lightness of the mood. She'd tried very hard not to go there, to avoid bringing it up.

"I don't think that's necessary." She started to walk away from him but he stopped her, his hand reaching for her arm. She moved so he couldn't restrain her. "I don't require explanations for something that is three years in the past."

"You do if you're under the impression that something happened between us."

She didn't remember. It was as simple as that. She had vague memories of leaving the hospital after visiting her father. She'd walked down the street to a restaurant. She remembered eating dinner, talking to a stranger, dancing. Ugh, she'd danced. In a crowded restaurant. She remembered Joe being there, his face hovering, him asking if she could walk. She put a hand to her face, wishing the memories away and yet wishing they were clearer, too.

As she stood there trying to force the memories forward, his phone rang. Tossing her an apologetic look, he pulled it from his pocket. The grimace that followed was comical. He silenced the phone and shoved it back in his pocket.

"You should have taken the call," she told him.

"It was my parents. I'll call them back later."

Interesting. "So, I'm not the only one avoiding a parent?" she asked.

"Not avoiding," he told her. The corner of his mouth tugged upward. "Okay, sort of avoiding. They want me to come home to Connecticut for Christmas. Which means they want to get me home and show me what I've been missing. I love them, but I don't miss that world. Imagine me in a suit, driving a sedan to some law office every day."

She could picture it. But in the image her mind created, he wore a cowboy hat with the suit. She told him that and he laughed.

"I should go inside," she said with reluctance that lived deep within.

"If I could, I would stay. I know this isn't easy for you." Joe's words were genuine. She knew that. But rather than seeing his face, this moment, she remembered her ex-husband and how he'd seemed like a person who wanted to protect her. In the beginning he'd been attentive, considerate, a real hero.

His gaze followed her hand, and she realized she'd touched the scarf at her neck. She pulled her hand away.

"I'm fine. Really. I'm going to talk to my dad. After all, that's why I came home." She opened the door. "You should go. Choir practice awaits."

"If you need me, call."

She put a hand to his shoulder. "I won't need you."

She wanted her past firmly in the past. That included Joe.

Daisy had promised Becky Stanford, the woman who had been like a second mother to her, that she would move forward, let go of the past, let go of her anger. She didn't know why Joe was on the list of things to deal with. Maybe because he was an unknown. Or perhaps it had to do with his loyalty to her father.

She knew that Joe's loyalty to Jack made him protective. Not just protective of Jack, but protective of her, too. She was an extension of Jack and not her own person.

It didn't matter. Joe hadn't been on her radar

when she made this move to Hope. He'd been a forgotten moment and she didn't need the distraction now, not when she was fulfilling her dream and creating this new life with a new purpose.

Chapter Three

Daisy waited until Joe drove away, then she turned to face her father. She walked through the door of the sitting room and paused to watch as her father cuddled a twin on each side, talking to them, making them laugh.

Maria had moved to her father's side and helped to hold the twins as Daisy's father played with them.

"They were fussing so we got them out," Maria explained. "I hope that's okay."

Daisy nodded but she didn't have words. She could only watch as Jack and Maria played with Myra and Miriam.

Vaguely she remembered this side of her father. Life might have been different if that had been the only side she'd known of Jack West. Unfortunately, she remembered the other side more. The side that had gotten lost in a bottle and would only climb out long enough to terrorize his family.

He looked up from the twins, his faded gray eyes reflecting compassion as he watched her enter the room, and take a seat in a chair as far removed from him as she could get.

"I'm glad you're home," he told her.

"Hope isn't really home," she said, knowing full well she sounded obstinate. She'd bought this place, officially making this—and Hope—her home.

His lips twitched. "Okay. Well, I'm still glad you're here. Why did you come back?"

"I'm not sure. I really just felt… I don't know." She stumbled over the words and then shrugged it off.

"I understand that. Sometimes we find ourselves on a path we hadn't anticipated." His eyes twinkled as he said it. "Enjoy the journey of discovery, Daisy. You might be surprised what you find."

She didn't know how to respond to that, or how she felt about being back. She only knew that she had to be here. Something had drawn her back to Hope, to her family, to this house.

"Maybe God wanted you here," Maria said with a hopeful expression. "Maybe you'll find yourself here."

Those words angered Daisy, but also made

her think back to a Sunday long ago when her Sunday-school teacher had taught a lesson about trusting God. *With God, all things are possible*, the teacher had told them as they colored pictures of Jesus and listened to a story about salvation. The story was meant to teach them that what looked impossible, through God was very possible.

She'd prayed that day, believing. Now she felt like the camel trying to fit back through that space where it didn't belong.

As she sat there with her father, with the twins, in this new home, the lesson from years past wouldn't leave her alone. It taunted her with images of a little girl who had desperately wanted to believe that when she prayed, those prayers would be answered.

"I think it might be too soon to talk about God," Jack said with insight that surprised Daisy. "Am I right?"

"Probably," she agreed. "God and I have had some misunderstandings. That wasn't what I wanted, but we don't always get what we want. In my case, I wanted you to be sober. And then I wanted my mom to see that her new husband was abusing her children. I won't make a list of all of my unanswered prayers."

"This is you coming home to take your future

into your own hands?" Jack said calmly, almost as if he approved.

"I suppose it is."

He nodded at that. "I'm glad. And I hope that in time, you'll find it in your heart to forgive me. I might disagree with you about faith and about prayer, but I won't disagree that we need a place to start fixing things."

"I'm working on forgiveness," she admitted. "But I need time."

"I'll give you all the time I have," he said.

His words shook her more than she would have liked to acknowledge. She watched him there with the twins, and she caught the way Maria's expression showed concern for him.

"What's your plan for this big old house?" Jack asked after a few minutes.

"I'm working on a plan."

He nodded, watching her, possibly seeing more than she would have liked. "If you need anything, I'm here."

"Thank you."

Myra moved from Jack's lap and slid to the floor, gaining her feet. The twins were almost a year old and hadn't yet decided to walk, but they were very mobile and into everything. At times it was exhausting, chasing the two of them. Myra grinned and took one step away from Jack before dropping to her knees and crawling to Daisy.

"She almost walked." Jack grinned as if it had been his proudest moment. He met Daisy's gaze. "About my foreman. How is it you and Joe seem to know each other so well?"

"We don't," she told him. "We've met a few times. At your surgery and again at each of my brothers' weddings."

"I guess I didn't realize you'd spoken."

"In passing," she answered.

Myra leaned against her, eyes growing heavy. "I should probably get them down for a nap."

Jack nodded, taking the hint. "I suppose you should. Is there anything Maria and I can do before we leave?"

"Not that I can think of." She stood and carried Myra to the playpen, and then she took Miriam from Jack's arms.

He had gained his feet while she put the twins down, covering them with a soft quilt a friend had made. Seeing Jack so unsteady did something inside her. She'd known for years that his health was slipping, but in her mind's eye, he'd remained strong, healthy, a giant of a man. And she'd thought she had plenty of time to make things right between them.

Now she wasn't so sure.

* * *

The twins napped for two hours. In that time, Daisy unpacked suitcases and explored the home that now belonged to her. She stood at the large windows and soaked in the familiar terrain of the town she'd grown up in. From upstairs she could see rooftops of the businesses and other homes. In the distance she could see the shimmer of water. The Grand Lake of the Cherokees was less than a mile from her house.

By the time the twins woke up from their nap, Daisy had realized how hungry she was and that she didn't have any groceries. Or a car. She did have a double stroller, part of their belongings Joe had delivered to her earlier in the day. She bundled up herself and the twins, although the day had warmed considerably, and headed out the door.

The walk to town was easy; just a few blocks and she was on Lakeside Drive. Her father and his philanthropy truly had changed this little town. And the town had changed lives. Not just the lives of veterans but the lives of longtime citizens and the people Jack had drawn to Hope to start new businesses.

Her sister-in-law Rebecca had come to Hope to open a hair salon and day spa. Her first day in town, Rebecca had met Daisy's half-brother,

Isaac. The two had fallen in love, married, and Isaac had adopted Rebecca's daughter, Allie.

It was hard to think about this new life her family had built. It was hard to imagine Isaac in the circle of her family. As children in Hope, Isaac hadn't been a brother, just a boy in town who looked a lot like the West siblings. After they'd gone away, Isaac had landed in Jack's home. His arrival had set Jack on his path to sobriety.

The circle of family had grown even more when Daisy's brother Colt had married Holly, the mother of his daughter Dixie. Dixie was the child the two had given up for adoption twelve years ago. Daisy had been in Dixie's life all these years because the girl had been raised by Becky Stanford. Colt and Holly were the ones Daisy felt closest to because they'd built a relationship with her in order to give their daughter stability. Dixie had spent part of the previous summer with Daisy, and through the fall, the twelve-year-old had spent the occasional weekend with her.

If anyone took the real credit for bringing Daisy back to Hope and into the lives of her family, it was her niece, Dixie. The young girl had helped Daisy realize how much it meant to have family.

One block from the café, a truck pulled alongside her, slowing to keep pace. She gave the driver an aggravated look, then realized it was Joe. He grinned and gave her a slight nod. Aggravating man! She continued on to the café and so did Joe. He pulled his truck into an empty parking space.

He headed her way with an easy smile and confident walk. Her gaze slipped from his face to his right arm that had been amputated from the elbow down. She dragged her attention back to his face.

Wrong move. He had dimples, the kind that were deep and obvious and made his smile more delicious than a man had a right to. Especially when coupled with dark eyelashes that made his hazel eyes more appealing. She bit the inside of her cheek to force her attention to something other than the many positive attributes of Joe Lawson.

She reminded herself that he was a "take charge" kind of man. He was probably overprotective. Those might seem like positive traits. Unfortunately, Daisy had seen the dark side of those things. Protective could quickly become possessive. Take charge could become controlling. There was a fine line. She knew how painful it could be when those lines were crossed.

When a man always seemed to be there, it

raised suspicions. It made the hair on the back of her neck stand up.

"Imagine seeing you here," he said as he joined her and the twins on the sidewalk.

"Is it a coincidence?" Her voice sounded strained. She drew in a breath. She didn't want to always be suspicious. She didn't want to live in fear.

"It's definitely a coincidence," he assured her. "I was at choir practice, and I'm heading to Holly's for a late lunch. Or early dinner. I'm not sure which, I only know that I'm starving. You?"

"I realized I don't have food or a car."

"You should have called me. I don't mind driving you to the store."

"I can walk. It isn't far."

"Do you mind if I walk with you and the girls?"

She stopped and gave him a look that didn't faze him. In response he smiled that lethal smile of his. She wasn't falling for it.

Never again would she be controlled, possessed or hurt. If she stayed in control, keeping people outside her personal space and controlling how much she let them into her life, she couldn't be hurt.

Before she could tell him all of that, his phone rang. He sighed as he looked at the caller ID.

"Might as well answer it and get it over with," she told him.

He nodded, then answered the phone. "Hi, Mom, how are you? Of course, go on in and I'll join you soon."

Daisy couldn't hear the other side of the conversation, but she supposed it wasn't a good sign when Joe brushed a hand over his face and faintly groaned. He looked up the street to Holly's Café. Curious, she followed his gaze and saw the group of people next to a large, black SUV parked in front of Holly's. Four people all waved. Joe put his phone back in his pocket.

"I take it your family decided to surprise you?" she asked, more than a little amused.

"You're finding this too funny," he practically growled.

"I thought you were always ready for anything that the world throws at you?"

"Not even close. My parents have come to visit. To make it more of a surprise, they brought my grandmother and my high school girlfriend."

She couldn't help but laugh. "That's not good. There's only one reason they would do that."

"To lure me back to Connecticut."

"Is it working?" she asked, curious. She didn't want to be curious. She didn't want to be anything when it came to Joe.

"No, it isn't working. Hope is my home now. I respect the fact that they'd like for me to come back and take a place in the family law firm. I just can't see myself in that world."

"How long will they stay?" she asked as they continued their walk.

"Just a few days. They visit a couple of times a year and stay at the Lakeside Resort. Dad and I go fishing. Mom shops. They go home disappointed that I choose to stay here."

"Be strong, cowboy. You've survived worse things."

"Thank you."

"I owed you a favor. The least I can do is be nice when your back is against the wall. Imagine, the great Joe Lawson afraid of a pretty blonde and a grandma."

"You're not helping," he said.

"I tried. Guess you're on your own. But I do think I'll head on into the café and watch the show."

She'd said that he was on his own. Alone was the last thing he felt at that moment. Something about having Daisy at his side felt comfortable. Although he should have thought things through a little more carefully. The two of them walking into the café together was sure to cause tongues to wag.

The same thought must have gone through her mind because she moved away from him as if he was suddenly contagious with the plague.

"My family is here, so I'll join them and I won't interfere with your family reunion." She hesitated. "But if you need anything…"

"Thank you," he responded, pushing his hat back on his head. "If I wave my hat, that means I need a rescue."

She ignored the joke, her attention on the table where the West family sat. Her smile disappeared, and he realized he wasn't the only one with tricky family dynamics.

"The same goes for you, Daisy. If you need a rescue, wave your hat."

That brought a hint of a smile to her face. "I don't have a hat so I'll have to wave a diaper."

He touched her back as a goodbye, and the two of them went their separate ways. As he walked away, he glanced back, just to check on her. He saw her hug Colt and then Dixie, Colt's daughter.

Joe couldn't put it off any longer. He circled tables, greeted the few people who were in the café for a late lunch and waved to Holly as he finally reached the table where his family waited. They got to their feet to greet him. His father, mother, grandmother and even Cassidy all stood up. His dad, Joe Senior, reached for his hand but then pulled him into a tight hug before letting him go. His mom, Marla, teared up a little as she wrapped her arms around him.

They were good parents, always had been. He had been blessed with a family that loved, supported and cared. His mom had cried when he told her about joining the army. His grandfather had been "highly disappointed."

The Lawsons were lawyers. It was in the DNA. Like their eye color, hair color and stature. Joe had dared to break from the family tradition. His parents had been so angry that they didn't write or call for several months after he left for his first duty station.

His grandmother, Eloise Lawson, had been his rock. She'd sent him many care packages. She'd called to wish him well. From the beginning she'd told him her heart ached, but her faith was strong that he would come home safe.

His grandmother was a class act. She could throw a dinner party, campaign for a senator, raise money for the hospital children's wing. She could also cook a mean fried bologna sandwich, change the oil in a car and keep a bunch of rowdy boys in line. Eloise Lawson had been raised by farmers in Kansas, but she'd met his grandfather, a law student, when she went off to college to earn her teaching degree.

He focused on his grandmother, smiling at

her as he tried to figure out the best way to proceed in what looked like treacherous terrain.

"Joe—" his dad motioned him to take a seat "—it's good to see you."

"We decided we would just have to come to you if you weren't coming to us." His mother, poised and beautiful, swiped away a tear. "I've missed you so much. Will your friend be joining us?"

His friend? For a moment he was confused. Of course they meant Daisy. He'd walked in with her. His parents had drawn a conclusion based on circumstantial evidence. He almost chuckled, but his grandmother had caught his eye. One of her gray brows arched in question.

"She's meeting her family for lunch," he responded to his mother's question.

"She's a local?" Cassidy finally spoke. Man, she was beautiful. The kind of beautiful that made a man feel as if he could never measure up.

He had been that man in her life. In his teen years, he'd been proud to have her on his arm but had soon been worn slick by her demands. She'd had him jumping through hoops to prove his love. At sixteen or seventeen he hadn't been ready for that kind of relationship. Back then, he also hadn't realized how unhealthy it was. As an adult, he got it.

"She's Jack West's daughter," he told her.

"And the babies?" Cassidy asked.

"They're twin girls." He didn't feel inclined to give details, since it was none of Cassidy's business.

The woman in question happened to be heading in his direction, looking determined and breathtaking. Loyalty to Jack had him backing away from that thought. The last thing he needed to do was go down that path. Daisy might be beautiful, but she was still Jack's daughter. Even friendship with Daisy would be complicated.

He didn't want to get tangled up in something that would hurt his relationship with Jack. Daisy West was off-limits.

Off-limits and yet she was smiling at him as if there was something more than a couple of chance meetings between them. She seemed to hesitate but she recovered quickly, pulling the smile back into place as she put a hand on his shoulder.

"Daisy?" He said it like the question it was. What was she doing? And why?

"Rebecca is watching the girls so I thought I'd come over so you could introduce me to your family." She gave them all a great, beaming smile that landed last on Cassidy.

Introductions? He opened his mouth, trying

to find the words, find a way to introduce the mysterious creature standing next to him, her hand moving from his shoulder to his back.

"Since Joe is speechless, guess I'll do the introductions. I'm Daisy West, his fiancée."

His mother gasped. His father looked shocked. Cassidy's expression changed from amused to outraged and his grandmother just laughed.

Joe sat there trying to figure out what had happened to the sane world he'd lived in just a day ago. An earthquake had struck, and he didn't know how to get his feet back under him. He only knew that he was being congratulated for an engagement to a woman who obviously didn't want any kind of relationship with him.

Chapter Four

Impulse control. For years Daisy had worked to keep a tight rein on her impulses. She didn't rush into anything. For example, it had taken her almost a year to go through with the sale of her business in Tulsa and the purchase of a house in Hope. Lack of impulse control had led her into several bad relationships, bad decisions and painful moments.

And yet here she was, standing in Holly's Café, Joe and his family in shock over what she'd just announced. She waited for Joe to deny the claim.

But instead of rejecting her, he reached up, taking her right hand in his left and bringing it close to his heart. He gave her hand a little squeeze, obviously asking silently what in the world she was thinking. She smiled down at him, not even sure how she would answer when the time came.

"Sit down so you can get to know my family." He had released her hand and pulled out the chair next to his.

She obviously hadn't given this enough thought. Or any thought. She sat, avoiding what she knew would be the bewildered looks of her family as they watched this scene unfold.

"How long have you been engaged?" Joe's father asked. His eyes narrowed on her, as if she were a specimen under a microscope.

"Not too long," Joe said off-handedly.

"Very recent." She smiled, the gesture feeling stiff. She felt cornered. But it was a corner of her own making.

There were more questions, more curious looks. Then the twins started to cry. She glanced their way, knowing Holly and Rebecca could handle the girls. At some point, Carson's wife, Kylie, had arrived. There were plenty of people to take care of Myra and Miriam.

Except Miriam was having none of it. Her cries grew louder.

"Go to her," Joe told her softly. "She wants you."

"I know. I'm sorry."

"Don't apologize." He winked, and she knew

that he meant more than her walking away to deal with Miriam. "We'll talk later."

"Of course we will," she managed to say in a soft voice. She apologized to his family and excused herself from their table. Slowly, dreading the conversation with her family, she walked across the café.

"What was that all about?" Isaac asked, sitting forward in his chair. Uncoiled, that was the best description for this half brother she'd only recently gotten to know as more than a childhood friend.

"None of your business," she told him.

He cocked his head to the side. "If that's the way you want to play this, fine. But I distinctly heard you claim an engagement to Joe."

She took Miriam from Kylie's arms and walked back and forth by the window, keeping her back to her curious family with all the questions. Questions they had every right to ask. Miriam quieted, her fingers playing with Daisy's hair as she sucked her thumb. Daisy kissed the baby's rosy cheek, then slowly turned to face her family.

Instead, she found that they'd all gone back to their own conversations and Joe stood behind her. He didn't look amused. She got that. She didn't feel too amused herself. She swallowed as she raised her eyes to meet his.

"Sorry," she whispered over Miriam's head.

He shook his head. "Let's go for a walk."

She nodded, knowing she couldn't refuse. The thing about being impulsive was that her actions always had to be dealt with. There were always consequences.

Isaac and Colt both looked up when she went to put Miriam in the stroller. Colt pushed his hat back and glared at Joe.

"Don't look at him like that," she warned her brother. "This is all me. And don't pretend either of you know me well enough to interfere in my life. You don't have that right."

Colt started to stand but Isaac pulled him back. "Let her go," Isaac told him. "Whatever it is, it'll work itself out. Joe doesn't look that unhappy about his situation. Maybe they've known each other longer than a day."

"We…" She started to say something, but Joe stopped her with a shake of his head.

"We actually *have* known each other longer than a day," Joe answered, flashing an easy smile that Daisy envied.

"Interesting," Colt said in a dangerously low voice.

Daisy refrained from sticking out her tongue. It would have been a juvenile thing to do. Picking up her purse, she left some money on the table and told her sister-in-law they needed to get together soon.

Holly came bustling from the kitchen. "Hey, I made you up a to go order. For you and the girls. And if you need to go to the store, let one of us know so we can give you a ride."

"I appreciate that. I'm supposed to get a rental car delivered soon, but in the meantime, thanks for the offer."

Isaac tipped his hat but shot Joe an ominous look. "Later," he said.

As they walked out the door, Daisy released a long sigh.

"I am so sorry," she told Joe as they walked down the sidewalk together.

The sun had come out and it was warm. This kind of warmth made her long for spring. It was the kind of day that had boats going out on the lake as die-hard fisherman searched out a good spot to catch a bass. The kind of day that had families in the park and people riding bikes along the many trails in and around the town of Hope.

"I don't know that I need an apology," Joe told her. "But an explanation would be a good start. Or even a plan, now that you have us engaged."

She groaned and shook her head. "I don't know what I was thinking. I saw you sitting with your family, and I knew how I'd feel. Cornered. Or ambushed."

"I could have handled it. Now I'm engaged." He chuckled, tossing her an easy, dimpled grin. "You put us from the pan to the fire with that move. What am I supposed to tell them when I don't have a wedding date? Or a wedding, for that matter."

"I got tired of your smug attitude and left you at the altar?" she asked, half teasing. "Where are we walking to?"

"I'm not sure. I guess the park."

"The park it is," she told him as she stopped at the crosswalk. "I can't believe this is the town of my childhood. When I lived here, twenty years ago, things were different. We had the grocery store, a few tired hotels by the lake and the feed store."

"And the rodeo grounds," Joe added.

"Right." She remembered riding her pony in the Under Ten age group for barrel racing. "I was teaching Dixie to ride before she came here to live with Colt and Holly. Her parents."

"That must have been hard, letting her go."

"I didn't let her go. She always belonged to them. And I still have her in my life."

Myra giggled from her seat in the stroller. Daisy smiled down at the girls. She tried not to think about losing them. Technically she wouldn't be losing them. A person couldn't lose what never truly belonged to them. Myra and Miriam belonged to their mother, Lindsey. They would always and forever be hers. Daisy got to borrow them for a short time, love them and hope that she made a difference.

"It'll be hard to let them go," Joe said.

They had reached the park, and Daisy positioned the stroller so she could sit on a bench and the girls would face her and Joe.

"It will be hard," she admitted. "I've been mentally preparing for that moment for a long time. I think they'll go home after the first of the year."

"That's pretty soon."

"It is. We have a court date next week. Lindsey has had several supervised visits. This time they'll determine a weekend for an unsupervised visit."

"I'm sorry," Joe said, reaching for her hand and giving it a light squeeze.

She nodded, for the moment, unable to speak. She opened the bag Holly had given her and found several containers within. One contained French fries. She pulled it out of the bag and put a few on the tray in front of the twins.

Finally she looked up, giving a slight shrug. "None of that has anything to do with you or what I've done to your life. I've complicated things. I'm sorry. You can tell your parents I lost my mind for a few minutes. Tell them I have a horrible sense of humor and that we aren't even friends, not really. Tell them I wanted to make your life difficult."

"That's a lot of options," he said. "Which one is true?"

She sat there, watching a couple with two little boys as they played together by the jungle gym. Envy plucked at her heart.

"Maybe a combination," she answered. "I *do* have a horrible sense of humor. I *did* want to mess with you."

"And the part about us not being friends?"

He gave her a sideways look as he lifted Myra from the stroller. "Come here, kiddo. You seem to be the female that likes me the most. Except maybe my Nana El. She's always liked me best."

"We are not enemies," she answered after a minute and a lot of thought. "Honestly, I don't know what we are."

"I'll take friendship," he told her. "Don't worry, I'm not holding you to this proposal."

She laughed and so did he, his laughter a slow rumble.

"Good thing. I'm afraid I'd leave you at the altar. The last thing I want is a real fiancé."

He pulled back a little. "I know I'm not the most handsome guy, but I'm a decent catch."

She ignored the comment about his looks. The last thing she wanted to admit was that when he smiled, she forgot herself just a little.

Instead, she said, "I don't go to church, Joe, but I do know about unequally yoked. I know that when you find someone, she's going to be a woman of faith. Someone decent and kind."

"*You're* decent and kind."

She rolled her eyes. "Thank you. But about our sudden engagement. If you want, I can confess and apologize to your parents."

"No, that isn't necessary." He sat the little girl on his lap and hooked his left arm around her. Miriam watched from the stroller.

"You can't mean to just let them think we're engaged. I'm definitely not going to play the part of your loving fiancée. I admit, I messed up."

"I'll tell them the truth," he told her.

"When? Seriously, Joe. We can't let people think we're engaged."

"Not even for a few days?" he teased.

"I can't believe you're even considering this!"

"They're going home Monday afternoon. Catching a flight out of Tulsa. We'll let it go because I don't see a reason to make a big deal out of this."

She had a feeling this was a very big deal. But only time would tell.

* * *

"Would you and the girls like a ride home?" Joe asked after sitting on the bench next to Daisy for a few minutes.

"You don't have to give me a ride." She settled both babies back in their stroller. "We're not really engaged, you know. I'm not going to expect flowers, candlelight dinners or any of the other things an engaged woman might expect."

"Stop! You're going to overwhelm me with your sweetness," Joe said dryly.

She opened her mouth to say something but then shushed him instead. He followed her gaze and saw what had her entranced. A dog. The same dog that had been roaming town for a couple of weeks. The animal was medium sized with a look of a sheep dog mixed with a hunting dog. Dark eyes peeked warily from hair that needed a trim and its ears perked up, either curious or sensing danger.

"She won't come to you," Joe warned. "Someone dumped her."

She wagged a finger at him. "Shhh."

He sat back and watched as she grabbed a few of the fries. She leaned down, calling to the dog. Her tone was soft, sweet, cajoling. It was a side of her that took him by surprise.

She was sitting next to him with twin baby girls whose mother had lost custody of them.

She'd claimed him as a fiancé in order to save him from his parents. Daisy West had a big heart. He'd always known her as Daisy, the abused wife, the wild child, the daughter who wouldn't come home, wouldn't forgive his mentor, Jack West.

Joe sat silently as she lured the dirty stray closer.

"Come on, sweet girl," she whispered gently. "You need to eat."

The dog half crawled to her, whimpering and submissive. It gobbled up the fries she'd dropped on the ground and Daisy sat still, not touching, waiting for the dog to come to her. It finally did. Of course it did. He was half ready to eat out of her hand himself.

She rubbed the dog's neck and called it the most precious animal ever. He had to disagree. The dog's coat was greasy and smelled less than fresh.

"Congratulations."

She smiled up at him, pleased. "Thank you. I always wanted a dog."

"You've never had a dog?" he asked.

"Never." She petted the dirty brown animal she'd befriended. "But now I have a dog."

"I'm not sure what to say," Joe told her. He glanced up as a drop of moisture hit the back of his hand, and he realized the park was deserted. "I do know that we should be going. I'll give you a ride home."

She glanced up at the sky, as if she hadn't realized the sudden change in weather, either. "What about my dog?"

"I'll give your dog a ride, too. But come on, before the rain really hits."

Daisy covered the girls as they dashed back toward the café where he'd left his truck. The dog followed them, as if she understood she'd found her person. She opened the front door of his truck and commanded the dog to get in.

"You just put that stinking dog in my truck!" Joe bellowed.

Her smile had him backing down. The truck could be cleaned after all.

She seemed to sense she'd won, and as he searched the truck for an umbrella, she hefted first one girl in a portable car seat and then the second, lifting them into the back of his truck. Once they were in, she climbed into the back seat to buckle them.

He grabbed what remained of the stroller and picked it up to place it in the back of the truck. The rain had calmed to a mist but the temperature had dropped drastically. He hurried to get inside.

The dog greeted him. Well, the smell of the dog greeted him. Joe climbed into his truck, pushing the animal to the passenger side. He glanced in the rearview mirror and made eye contact with Daisy.

"I can say that being engaged to you is not going to be dull." He shifted into Reverse and pulled out onto the road.

"I've never been accused of being boring," Daisy quipped.

They were pulling in to her driveway when his phone rang. His mom's name appeared on the display. He glanced back again and Daisy waved.

"Might as well get it over with," Daisy said encouragingly.

He answered.

"Joe, it's Mom."

"Hi, Mom," he answered as he looked to the rearview mirror again. Daisy had a twin on each side of her.

"I thought I'd let you know, Dad and I talked. We're going to church in the morning. I know, we don't usually do that. But we thought it would be a good idea. After all, our son is the choir director."

"Not the choir director, Mom. I sing in the choir."

"I know, I just… I didn't know you even liked to sing."

"I was in choir back in high school."

She laughed at that. "Yes, of course you were. Well, we'd like to go to church and then have lunch with you and your fiancée. And her little girls."

From the back seat he heard Daisy gasp. He shot her a warning look.

"I'll have to check with Daisy," he told his mother.

"I understand. It would just be nice if we could get to know her better."

"Of course. I'll see you tomorrow."

The call ended.

"I'm not going to church!" Daisy informed him. Her smile had dissolved, and her mouth was set in a determined line. "No way."

"I know you're not. I'll come up with an excuse why you can't be there."

They spent the next few minutes in silence. Joe drove to her house and pulled up to her front door. The rain had eased up and the wind had calmed down. Joe glanced to the back seat.

"I'll come around and help you all out."

Daisy ignored him. She looked across the street at the neighboring houses. Finally she looked at him, as if remembering his presence.

"I'll go to church," she told him in a quiet voice.

"You will?" he asked. "In exchange for what?"

"You have to help me decorate for Christmas. I need a tree. And I'd like outside lights. The girls are little, but it's their first Christmas. I want them to have a wonderful holiday. Even if they don't remember it, I will. I'll remember that we gave them a special day."

He felt her words like a punch to the gut. She feared losing the girls. She'd done this for their mother. She'd known it was the right thing to do for them. And soon, in the next few months, she would have to say goodbye to Myra and Miriam. The idea unsettled him.

In that moment, he'd have given them—and her—anything he possibly could in order to make their day special.

"I'll help you." He didn't have to promise. There was no way he would tell her no. Not when it meant a Christmas for her and the girls.

"Thank you, Joe."

He jumped out of the truck, opened the back door and the dog jumped out. It immediately ran to her front porch, as if this house had always been her home.

"I guess you have a dog now," he told Daisy.

"I guess I do."

When they were all inside, Joe stood at the door, knowing he had to go. He pulled off his hat and wiped moisture from his face. Daisy looked up at him, and something about that look set him back on his heels. Joe met her gaze and she shrugged, as if unsure.

"Would you like some coffee?" she asked.

"Thanks, but I should go."

"It's raining and you're soaked and it's because you had to drag us home and help us get inside." She rambled, shifting to glance at the room where the twins played on a blanket. "A cup of coffee is the least I can do."

"We don't have to keep paying each other back, Daisy," he told her. "I can do a favor without a favor done in return."

"That's good to know." She put a hand to the scarf at her neck. "Joe, I don't give my friendship easily. I don't trust just anyone."

"I know." The air around them grew heavy. His hand went to the doorknob because he knew he should walk away.

But he couldn't.

She loosened the scarf. The scar was a vivid and puckered streak of red across her neck. "My husband tried to kill me," she whispered.

He'd known, but until this moment the event had been removed from his life. Daisy had been a stranger that he'd once helped. She hadn't been real. In two days she'd become more. She was a person with the heart and courage to raise twin baby girls. A woman who would brashly claim to be his fiancée. A woman who could lure in a stray dog that everyone in town had tried to befriend.

He'd never expected to feel rage at the man who was now in prison, wishing he could put him in prison all over again. Or worse.

"I only wanted you to know, I don't give my trust easily." She told him a second time.

"I know you don't," he said. He valued the gift of her friendship, the trust that wasn't easily given. "And I hope this makes us friends."

"It makes us friends. But please don't hurt me."

He leaned toward her, brushing a kiss to her forehead.

"I'll do my best."

Then he left, because that seemed like the safest thing to do. Daisy West had taken him by surprise, shifting his world a little off-kilter. Not for the first time. But for some reason, this time felt a little more dangerous.

Chapter Five

Daisy stood at the door of the church nursery, watching as a woman named Anna cuddled Miriam, who looked perfectly happy. She'd expected it from Myra. The more outgoing of the two, she'd immediately started playing. Both twins seemed okay, but Daisy didn't want to walk away.

She didn't want to go down the hall to the door that led to the sanctuary. She knew the way. She'd been here numerous times as a child. But her feet wanted to stay planted where she stood. Her feet, joined by her heart, didn't want to go down and face whatever lay at the end of the hallway.

Kylie sidled up next to her. "Want to walk with me? It isn't easy the first time but it gets easier, I promise."

"I'm not…" She stopped herself from saying

something about not coming back again. But she didn't want to offend her sister-in-law.

Kylie didn't push. Carson's wife had always been sweet. In school she'd been a couple of grades ahead of Daisy, but even then, she'd been kind. She'd been a friend, as much as young girls can be at that age.

There was a long silence between them as they walked back to the sanctuary. No doubt that Kylie wanted to ask about the engagement. But she wouldn't. It wasn't Kylie's way to pry.

"How are you and the girls settling in to the new house?" Kylie asked.

"It's only been a few days, but so far we're doing well."

"I'm glad to hear that. Will you please call if you need anything?"

"I promise to call. But I really can handle most things on my own."

"I know you can," Kylie responded. And then she lifted a finger to her lips as they neared the open door of a classroom. She stopped, pulling Daisy to a stop next to her and put a finger to her lips.

From inside the room, the children's voices raised in a Christmas hymn, then one of the boys walked up to a microphone to speak. "And then the angel said, 'For behold, I bring you great titles of joy that shall be to all nations. For a baby is born and this shall be assigned to you, you will find the baby wrapped up in swatting clothes and a lion in a manger.'"

The teacher, obviously trying to hide her laughter at the mistakes, stepped forward. She gave the little boy a quick hug and told him he'd done a fantastic job. They needed to work on only a few words while the other children practiced singing "Away in a Manger."

Kylie pointed to a girl at the edge of the group, her smile wide. Carson's daughter, Maggie. She saw them and waved. Daisy's heart filled up with love for her niece. This little girl and her brother Adam were two of the reasons she'd come home.

The children began to sing. Maggie's voice was distinct. Daisy could pick it out from the others. It was sweet and still childlike. It was precious to her. She closed her eyes briefly and imagined Christmas with family. Christmas with more than a dinner out with her employees. More than a small tree on a card table with just a few gifts for Becky and Dixie.

She thought about the twins and the joy of watching them see the lights, play with gifts, laugh as they were passed from person to person. And then in her mind's eye, she saw how her life would be without them.

She wasn't sure she liked it.

"We should go," Kylie whispered, pulling her back from where her mind had gone.

The two of them made their way to the sanctuary where pews were beginning to fill. The church had been decorated with poinsettias, a nativity scene on a table near the front, twinkling lights.

It had been a long time since she'd been in church, but she wondered if the Magi had seen the star and followed it for the same reason, because of what they'd been told, about the birth of a savior. Not that these decorations were comparable to that star. She couldn't imagine something that would send her on a journey like those men had taken.

But then, here she was, on her own journey. And wasn't she searching for something, too?

Joe Lawson stood, leaving his family to approach her. He was exactly the opposite of what she was searching for. He represented everything she meant to avoid. She was searching for peace and closure.

He'd already brought a lot of confusion to her life.

When he reached her, she tried her best to smile. "What are you doing?" she asked him.

His grin wasn't fake, pasted on or tense. It was heartwarming in a way that made her angry.

"I'm your fiancé," he said easily. "I thought we should sit together."

Mysteriously, Kylie had disappeared. There would be no escaping this moment. After a long pause, she said, "Of course."

She'd made this bed. Now she had to lie in it. But it had fleas. Possibly bed bugs.

He took her by the hand.

"Don't fight it," he teased.

She drew in a breath at the words, reminding herself that this was Joe and not her ex-husband. He must have sensed what was happening because his grip on her hand loosened and he put space between them. When she glanced up, there was concern in his expression.

"I'm fine," she said.

"Are you?"

"Of course." Another fake smile.

They finally made it to the pew where his family waited for them. People all around were getting seated for the service. The pastor had moved to the pulpit. Joe sat next to his mother and Daisy sat next to him, thankful to be on the aisle.

A few pews ahead, she saw her father sitting with Maria, Carson, Kylie and their children. Ahead of them, Isaac and Rebecca sat with Allie and their new baby. Next to them, there was Colt, Holly and Dixie. The girl turned to wave at her, her smile as wide as the Mississippi. She whispered to Colt and he nodded. Suddenly Dixie was hurrying to Daisy's side.

"What are you doing?" Daisy asked.

"Giving you a hug. You look like you needed one." Dixie grabbed her and squeezed hard, then hurried back to her seat.

She hadn't changed a bit. Daisy's heart warmed at the thought. She wanted nothing but the best for the girl who had been such a huge part of her life. As she watched Dixie with her parents, Daisy was content, knowing she was happy and loved. Watching them all together also helped take her mind off her own nervousness.

The sight of them got her through the music, through Joe's arm brushing against hers. It got her to the sermon framed around the book of Isaiah and the prophecies of the birth of the savior.

Then her phone buzzed. She glanced at the caller ID and ignored the call. It buzzed again a few moments later. Joe looked at her, arching a brow in question.

"The twins' mom," she whispered. "I have to take it."

He nodded. She slipped out of the pew and exited through the main doors. Outside the sun shone bright but the air was cool, with a sharp breeze that went right through her sweater. She moved to the side of the building for shelter.

"Lindsey, what's up?"

"How are my girls?" Lindsey asked, her voice a little too bright. "I miss them. I wish you hadn't moved so far away."

"I'm not that far, and you'll still see them."

"I know. I know." She paused. A long and troubling pause.

"Lindsey?"

A sniffle on the other end. "I had a random drug test. It was random. They shouldn't have done it. They just didn't warn me."

"Lindsey." Daisy wanted to cry because she knew what was coming next.

"Yeah, well, I mean, I didn't *do* anything. I was just around people, and they were using."

Lies. Addicts always lied.

"You know it doesn't work that way." Daisy couldn't hide her disappointment. The other woman had been clean for six months. She was so close to reuniting with the girls. "Why now?"

"I don't know. I was with the wrong people."

"Also your choice."

"My girls mean everything to me."

Daisy had to count to ten. Twice. "Then make choices that show they mean everything."

"Yeah, I know. Well, my lawyer will no longer represent me. He's court appointed but he said he's done with me."

Daisy leaned against the side of the building, eyes closed. Praying? No, she wasn't going to pray. But maybe she'd exhausted every other avenue of help. Maybe God was the safety net when everything else had failed.

She chastised herself. It was wrong to use God as a crutch when all else failed. Then again, she'd always been an all or nothing type of person.

For years she'd preferred nothing. Not counting on anyone else. She didn't allow other people to let her down.

"Daisy, I'm sorry. I want my girls. I do. I'm going to get this right."

"I know," she said weakly, trying to give the other woman, once a friend, the encouragement she needed.

How could this happen to someone she knew? A woman who had worked hard to build a better life for herself? A woman who was smart, full of potential, able to succeed at anything she put her mind to?

One wrong choice. One wrong friendship. One wrong relationship. Everything Lindsey had ever wanted and worked for was on the other side of a huge chasm again. She needed a lifeline to get back to who she had been.

"I'm still here, Lindsey. But I can't make decisions for you. You have to do this for yourself and your daughters."

"I know."

They had court on Thursday. Court with a positive drug test and no lawyer. She didn't need to tell Lindsey how bad this looked for her.

"You'll be here Thursday? I can visit my girls with you to supervise."

"I'll be there. But I have to go now. I'm at church."

"Oh. Okay. I'll let you go." Then the line went dead. Daisy leaned against the side of the church, stared up at the impossibly blue sky and tried to figure out how to trust and how to separate God, faith and the people who had hurt her in the name of religion.

Suddenly Joe appeared in front of her. Tall and steady, and somehow in her life. Her choice, she reminded herself. Her impulsive words had placed him here, thinking he had a right to stand there with questions in his eyes. For some reason it didn't really bother her.

He'd breached her defenses. There should be some type of warning siren, telling her to take shelter. She smiled at the thought.

"You okay?" he asked.

She shook her head. "Nope. Not really. The

twins' mom. She had a random drug test and tested positive."

Shrugging, she tried to pretend it didn't really hurt.

"The house was born of some crazy idea that I could buy a place and help women who've been abused, who've made bad choices. They could find hope in Hope. I want to call it Faith House, for a friend who didn't get away, who didn't make it." Her voice broke, remembering the woman she'd met in a support group for abused wives.

Faith had gone back to her husband. At her funeral, Daisy had made a decision to do something more than attend a group. Some women wanted out; they just had nowhere to go.

"Her positive drug test doesn't mean this can't work or that your dream for this house is dead." Joe rubbed his right elbow. "I spent a few hard months thinking I wouldn't be able to do anything. My life was framed by this amputation and all the ways I thought it would limit me. What I learned is that I was the one limiting myself. God gave us a purpose in this life. It sounds as if you've found yours."

"Thank you," she whispered, brushing away the dampness that had trickled down her cheek. She stood on tiptoe and kissed his cheek. "I mean that. I should probably go get the twins."

"Kylie is getting them for you. She also said to let you know there's a committee meeting for a Christmas fundraiser. She has to stay at church for a few extra minutes and she'll be late getting to Mercy Ranch for lunch."

"What's the fundraiser for?" she asked, eager to focus on normal, everyday things.

"Christmas for the Community. The church raises funds for a big dinner that's held the Sunday before Christmas. It's a community event. Every child receives a gift. There are also new coats, winter boots, gloves and hats for those who need them."

"Faith in action," she acknowledged. "I like it."

She stepped away from him, because this all felt too easy, too comfortable. "I have to get the twins from Kylie."

"I'll see you back at the ranch," he said, giving her space to leave.

The entire West family met for lunch at Mercy Ranch every Sunday after church. Even better, Joe's family had been invited this afternoon.

What a tangled web she'd created for herself.

Joe didn't like the melding of his two worlds. Having his family and Cassidy at Mercy Ranch made him a little itchy. He truly loved his parents. Always enjoyed their visits. Typically, he knew how to handle them when they pushed for him to return to Connecticut.

Most people would probably jump at the life he'd been born to. He'd never worried about his future. He'd grown up with every advantage. Right now he could be back in Connecticut, whole and unharmed. A partner in the family law firm. And he thrown it all away, according to his father.

He preferred to think he traded it for something that suited him better. The Army had suited him. And now this life in Hope suited him. This life, he never would have known it if he hadn't made his own choices. His future would be far different from anything his parents ever thought to plan.

And Cassidy was not part of that future.

Although at the moment, she stood next to him, her hand on his arm, her shoulder leaning close to his. Pulling away would have been too obvious so he stood next to her in Jack West's dining room, talking to his dad, nodding in Isaac's direction and waiting for Daisy to arrive.

The strange sensation that rippled through him couldn't be anticipation. He rubbed his chest with his left hand. Heartburn? He felt suspiciously like a kid at Christmas, eagerly anticipating opening Christmas gifts.

He'd been settled in his life here for several years. Content. It had been a long, long time since he'd felt these other emotions. Like there was something on the horizon, something new and unknown.

The truck Jack had loaned Daisy pulled up to the house. He excused himself and went out to help her with the twins. She got out of the truck and opened the back door.

"Is the house on fire?" she asked as he walked up to her. "Or maybe the fair Cassidy is taking advantage of my absence and making her move?"

"The house is *not* on fire," he assured her as he took Myra out of her car seat and circled to the other side of the truck where she was unbuckling Miriam. "Are they identical?"

"You know they are. Stop trying to change the subject. Should I feel threatened by the old girlfriend?" she teased.

"Not at all," he assured her, and meant it.

She shot him a questioning look. And he guessed he should say something teasing to lighten the mood. But he didn't.

Together they walked to the back door. Isaac saw them coming and held the door open for them. "Look at the happy family."

"Look at me pushing you off the porch," Daisy teased. She even smiled when she said it.

Joe wanted to hug her.

Everyone was lined up at the buffet of food that Maria had prepared along with Kylie, Rebecca and Sierra St. James. Sierra and her husband Max spent every other Sunday with their Mercy Ranch family. Joe watched the two of them together, happy that Sierra had found joy and had grown stronger with Max in her life.

Kylie smiled and made a beeline for Daisy. "I have high chairs set up for the twins. Rebecca got their plates all ready, so the food could cool."

"Thank you," Daisy looked perplexed. "I'm sorry, I'm just used to doing this all by myself. I really appreciate the help. And the break."

"Of course you do," Kylie laughed as she took Myra from Joe. "All moms think they can do it on their own. But we need help and a break from time to time. I've never had little ones, but even Maggie and Adam can give me a run for my money."

Joe tried to eavesdrop on their conversation, but he overheard his dad talking to Jack. Daisy must have also heard them because she glanced their way. Something about a house on the lake.

"We were able to rent it through the end of the year," his father was telling Jack. "It's on the market and, who knows, we might decide to buy it. But this will give us a chance to spend more time with Joe and to get to know Daisy. I think our daughter and her husband will fly in for Christmas."

The floor dropped out from under Joe. He heard a sharply indrawn breath and couldn't tell if it came from him or from Daisy. He only knew that Rebecca appeared and Miriam was promptly removed from Daisy's arms.

He and Daisy stood there in the center of the room, no doubt both wearing "deer in the headlight" looks on their faces. Colt walked past him, giving him a firm pounding on the back.

"Have you taken Daisy out to see that new foal yet?" Colt asked. "Joe had to help the mare out," he told Daisy, "but the baby came yesterday and she's a fine little filly."

"We're having lunch right now," Jack said to his youngest son. Isaac and Colt were half-brothers and they'd been born around the same time. In the same town. It had been quite the scandal, or so he'd heard.

To Joe, it was proof that some people could change. Some people could put down the bottle and make a different life for themselves. Jack had come a long way, and he admired him endlessly for it.

Daisy reached for his hand. "We won't be long."

Out the door they went, Daisy practically

dragging him by his hand as they walked across the patio. The stable was several hundred feet from the main house. Jack had built quite a ranch for himself. From the tumbledown farmhouse he'd once called home, now renovated as a residence for men like Joe, had come this place. This dream for rebuilding lives.

"It's quite a stable," Daisy said as they walked. The dog, Mutt, joined them. More dogs barked from the kennel where Kylie trained service animals, wanting to make their presence known. Horses grazed in the field. On the opposite side of the barn, cattle moved along a line of hay that had been rolled out for their morning meal.

"It is pretty fantastic," Joe told her. "But it's time for me to move to my own place. Jack and I have talked about it."

"But not back to Connecticut," she said.

"No. I won't be going back to Connecticut. I'm going to open a small law office here in Hope."

"Living the dream," she teased.

"I have a good life here."

"And now a fiancée. We need to stop this. How do we stop this?"

"Yeah, I don't know. I didn't expect them to stay through Christmas."

"I know you didn't. You also didn't expect to be engaged. To me."

He had to laugh. "That did take me by surprise. Thanks for trying to rescue me. But I'll let you off the hook. I know this isn't what you bargained for."

They stepped through the side door of the stable, into the warm and shadowy recesses of the building. Only a few horses were stabled. A stallion who had a corral that he could go to for exercise, a mare that was close to foaling and the mare who had just foaled. The stable had the capacity to house a dozen horses. There was also a shelter in the field and a smaller barn with several stalls. Jack took care of his livestock, horses and cattle. Oh, and the llama he'd bought at an auction.

"I'm not your fiancée" Daisy spoke softly as she reached through the bars to pet the stallion Jack had recently purchased. The big red quarter horse whinnied and nuzzled her hand.

"I think we both know that," Joe assured her. "I'm pretty sure all of your family is aware that this isn't real."

She pulled her hand back and moved on to the mare and foal. "She's a beauty. If you need me to continue this until your family leaves, I will."

"An engagement of convenience?" he gibed as he opened the stall door. The mare moved forward, her foal staying close to her side.

"That's only for romance novels. And I'm not

sure if this is okay. I feel like your parents just want what's best for you. Are you sure that isn't Cassidy?"

"I know she isn't. I'm not sure why she's here or what they all think, but I've never been the person she wants. I'm not quite handsome enough or polished enough. I'm no longer a suit and tie kind of guy. When we dated in high school, I was just the guy who took her to dinner and opened doors for her. Nothing more."

"I see." She stepped into the stall and stood close to the mare. "I mean, I still need those Christmas decorations put up in and around the house. And now, it seems I need a lawyer for the twins' mother."

"Is this extortion?" He found it hard to be offended. She had that innocent look on her face, but her silver-gray eyes sparkled with mirth.

"I mean, maybe," she laughed. "I consider it more of a trade. You need a fiancée. I need help."

"You're beautiful when you barter," he found himself saying. The words took them both by surprise. "And I'm rarely impulsive."

"Maybe you should be impulsive more often?"

He liked that idea. "Maybe so."

Then he took her advice to heart and brought her closer to him with his left arm, wishing like crazy he could caress her face. No sense wishing for what could never be. Instead, he touched his lips to hers. For a moment she kissed him back, raising a hand to his neck.

Only for an instant and then she stepped back. "That isn't part of the deal, cowboy."

He raised his left hand, surprised by his own behavior.

"I know it isn't. It…" He faltered. He wasn't going to lie to her. He also wasn't about to back her into an emotional corner. "It won't happen again. I know…"

She drew in a breath and her hand touched her neck, to the scarf she always wore. She pulled it loose. "You don't know. I have scars deeper than this one, but I'm tired of living my life in fear that I'll make the same mistake a second time. I like you, Joe, and you seem to be a decent and good man but I can't remember that night, so maybe you aren't."

The night he took her home. He dragged his gaze back to her face, away from the scar that she kept covered with the scarf. He wanted to erase her past, make her feel safe and unafraid. But he couldn't. It wasn't his place.

"I took you home, Daisy. End of story. I wish you had called me. We could have talked. I was worried about you so I took you home. I locked the door, and I left a note next to your keys."

She hung her head. "That was not my best night. I was so lost, so afraid for my dad, but also so angry at him."

"We all make mistakes."

"Including you?"

"Yes, including me." He backed up and let her leave the stall.

She walked away from him, stopping when she got to the door.

"I don't want to be hurt again," she told him without turning.

"I don't plan on hurting you," Joe assured her. He started toward her but decided against it. She needed space.

"I don't trust easily," she said, shifting only slightly, to show him the side of her face.

"I know."

She nodded once, then walked out the door.

A moment later he followed, because he couldn't not follow. She'd turned his life upside down. She made him question everything, even his own life choices.

Several years ago, he had realized the truth in Philippians 4, that it meant trusting God, no matter what your situation. Like the apostle Paul, Joe guessed he knew a little about being content in his circumstances. Paul had put it best. He knew how to live with plenty and how to be content with next to nothing. He knew where his strength came from. It came from his faith.

Now he didn't know what came next, and he sure didn't like the feeling of facing the unknown.

Chapter Six

"How long are you going to avoid me?"

Joe started at the voice but that was nothing compared to the reaction of the horse he'd just cross-tied in the center aisle of the stable. The big bay stomped his back leg and kicked a little. Enough to make Isaac West take a step back.

Joe quieted the horse, talking softly and smoothing his hand down the horse's neck. He glanced back at Isaac but didn't have an answer to the question he'd been asked. He hadn't really been avoiding Isaac.

True, it was Tuesday and they hadn't really talked since Sunday, but that wasn't avoiding. It just meant they'd been busy. Didn't it?

"Billy, can you bring me the bridle?" Joe called out to the young man who had recently moved to Mercy Ranch, a marine who had grown up on a farm in Virginia but nightmares and a broken body were keeping him from returning to that life and to the fiancée who clearly wanted him home.

"Not talking to me?" Isaac asked as he moved closer.

The horse shifted his back end, and Joe pushed to keep him in place.

"I'd prefer you to stop talking, actually." Joe continued to calm the horse. "You know this horse's history. Trust isn't an easy thing to gain, and you seem to think you have to keep talking to get the answer you want."

"Not all of us can keep that perfectly regulated tone of yours, Joe," Isaac continued, a little softer, though. "Still can't get him to take a bit in his mouth?"

"Someone must have done a number on him. Head shy and startles at everything. I'm not going to force him. I'm giving him time to realize I'm not the enemy."

It sounded as if he was talking about someone other than the horse. Someone like… Daisy. He wanted her trust. He wanted her to know that he wouldn't hurt her, not intentionally. Not if he could help it.

He could admit he didn't know where all of this was leading. He only knew one thing: he had to trust that God had a plan. Maybe the plan was for Joe to help Daisy reconnect with her family. Maybe the plan was for him to help with her home or even with the twins and their mother.

He was definitely in her life to help her in some way. He liked that idea. Embraced it, actually.

"I'm not the enemy, either." Isaac moved under the rope to Joe's left, causing the horse to shift sideways. Now the unruly West brother stood behind him, and Joe had to shift to face him.

"No, you're not the enemy, but you're quickly becoming a pain. I'm working here." He drew in a breath and made an attempt to calm down. The horse sidestepped, his shod hoof coming down hard on Joe's foot.

He jumped back, nearly swearing at the pain of having a twelve-hundred-pound animal land on his foot. He limped to a bench and sat down, then shot the laughing Isaac a look.

"You happy now?" Joe said as he yanked off his boot.

Isaac shrugged.

"Billy, brush him down and once he's calm, work on the bridle. Without getting hurt."

Billy, usually a pretty quiet guy, seemed to be working hard to keep from laughing. "Yes, sir."

"I'm not your sir," Joe seethed. "Give the

horse a carrot and apologize to him for Isaac's crass way of handling animals and people."

"Sure thing, boss." Billy picked up the brush Joe had dropped and went to work.

Joe grabbed his boot, pushed to his feet and limped down the aisle of the stable to the office. Isaac, of course, followed close behind him.

"You could just force the bit in his mouth and let him get used to it. Eventually he'll see it isn't hurting him," Isaac offered as they entered the office. "And then you could focus on telling me what kind of game you're playing with my sister."

Joe grabbed a bag of frozen peas out of the office fridge's freezer. They kept a supply of the frozen vegetables on hand for moments like this. He sat down at the desk and propped his foot up, dropping the bag on the bruised portion.

"You used to be tougher," Isaac said as he poured himself a cup of coffee and sat down. "Oh, do you want coffee?"

"No, I don't want coffee. I also don't want your advice on handling that horse. You know that's the worse advice ever. Cut to the chase and tell me what you want."

"I told you. What kind of game are you playing with my sister?"

"No game." He moved the bag of frozen

peas and studied his foot. "It's between me and Daisy."

"That's not the truth. Maybe if you'd picked any other woman you could say that. But you picked a woman with three brothers."

"Shaking in my shoes, Isaac." Joe leaned back in the chair.

From the open door, he could hear Billy talking to the horse, calling it something ridiculous. If the kid wanted to call the horse Queen Elizabeth, Joe wouldn't care. Not if it helped Billy heal.

Broken horses and broken people went hand in hand, fixing each other. That was Jack West's philosophy at Mercy Ranch. It took time but it usually worked out. In this situation, Joe thought the horse was further ahead than Billy. He kind of thought Big Red was playing along, giving Billy something to work on.

Isaac tested the coffee, made a face, then took another swig. They'd both been listening to Billy. Isaac's face showed he cared, even if he wanted to play gruff and tough to the bitter end. "This stuff is awful."

"You're the one who buys the coffee for the barn." Joe moved his foot to the floor and reminded himself that Isaac had been his friend for several years. They'd gone through some stuff together. They'd sat up nights, reliving their time in Afghanistan, the things they'd seen and done and getting past the nightmares. A man didn't share that kind of past without learning to trust. "I'm asking you to trust me."

"I trust you. It's just...she's Daisy. And even if I'm the brother with the least claim on her, I care. I care that she's been hurt in the past. I care for her sake and for Jack, because he wants her here. He needs to resolve their past and find peace with her."

"I don't plan on hurting her." He glanced at his watch, hoping to shift the conversation to something less complicated. "I guess you know I signed the contract on that property."

"Yeah, I do know. I'm excited for you but not so excited for us."

"Jack never planned for the residents of the ranch to stay here on a permanent basis. We come here to heal and start over. Time for me to move on."

"You're like part of the family." Isaac chuckled. "And not because you announced some sham engagement to get your folks off your back."

"Sham engagement!"

"Oh, come on, we're friends. I know you too well. For years you've avoided anything that looks like a relationship. My sister showing up here has nothing to do with whatever half-baked idea you came up with when you saw your parents and their chosen bride for you."

"I'm not avoiding relationships," Joe countered. "I'm taking my time and waiting for God to bring someone into my life. You of all people should get that."

"Yeah, well, this doesn't look like waiting for God to me."

Joe met his friend's steady gaze. "I won't hurt her."

Isaac finished off his cup of coffee and stood. "I'm heading to the church. I'm supposed to be in charge of the Christmas dinner. Are you still heading up the quartet for Christmas music?"

"Yes, unless someone has decided otherwise. And we've nearly doubled the amount of toys we collected last year."

Isaac grinned. "You'll make a nifty Santa."

"Nifty?" He blinked, just realizing what Isaac had said. "I'm not Santa."

"Kids like you, Joe. I know you look like a giant Grinch and you growl like Scrooge, but there's something kind of cuddly about you."

"Go," Joe said.

Isaac hurried to the door. "A little frightening but mostly warm and fuzzy."

Joe growled. After Isaac left, a trail of laughter following him, Joe dug out a package he'd picked up early that morning when he'd gone to the feed store for a cup of coffee and the local gossip.

Two toy mangers, just right for tiny hands. They were made of rubber and were soft and even safe to chew. The mangers were perfect for the twins. When he'd seen them at the feed store with other similar toys, he hadn't been able to resist.

The men who'd been gathered around the store's wood-burning stove drinking their morning coffee hadn't been able to resist teasing him as he'd made the purchase. He'd tried to convince them the toys were for the church toy drive. No one had believed him.

He'd been thinking about Daisy and the twins, and maybe that meant he ought to visit them and deliver the toys. He pulled his boot back on his foot, grimacing as he shoved his heel down into the soft leather. He'd kind of exaggerated the pain for Isaac's benefit. But he wasn't exaggerating as he limped out of the office and down the aisle of the stable, telling Billy he'd be in town if anyone needed him.

A few minutes later he pulled up in front of the house on Prairie Rose Drive. All was quiet as he got out and headed for the front door. A soft woof greeted him. The dog had stayed. Not only had he stayed, but he had a soft bed on the porch and fancy bowls with food and water. Daisy obviously intended to keep the animal.

Joe patted the dog's head, then raised his hand to knock on the door. From inside he could hear a child's cries. One of the twins was not happy. He knocked, waited several seconds and knocked again. No one answered.

A moment later he heard two children crying. He tried the doorknob. It twisted and he pushed it open.

"Daisy? You here? Everything okay?" Joe walked through the house, the dog following close behind him.

The two of them followed the crying, which led them to the family room at the back of the house. Daisy shot up from the chair where she sat cuddled with both babies. The babies were in diapers and nothing else. Daisy's shirt was inside out. Her hair had been pulled back in a haphazard ponytail.

He tossed the toys on a nearby table. "What can I do to help?"

"Please take them so I can get cleaned up. They…" She shuddered. "I don't know what to do. They're both sick and…"

The smell of vomit reached him and he made a face.

"Do not. Don't you dare." Daisy stood in front of him, appearing smaller than she was. She lifted her chin to give him a rather fierce glare. "I did not sign on for this."

"I don't think anyone signs on for this." He kept his mouth in a firm line.

"Do not laugh," she warned. "I haven't slept. And I'm starting to feel sick myself. This isn't a good day."

"I'm not laughing. This is not a laughing matter. I'm a rancher. I can handle this. Let me take them."

"You're sure? I know you have things to do. A family to visit."

"I've got this." He held his breath as he lifted the twins from her arms. "Go get cleaned up. We'll be fine."

She moved a safe distance from him. "You think you're fine. You have no idea. It's like something from a scary movie."

He tried to stand there without breathing. It was impossible. He gasped for air, took a deep breath and tried to think of something encouraging to say.

Daisy laughed, the sound mixing with relief. She put a hand to her mouth and shook her head before running to the bathroom.

Joe looked down at the twins he held, trying to decide what to do next. "You're both kind of gross, you know that? I hope it doesn't ruin your self-esteem when you're older. Honestly, I know you'll both grow up to be very sweet human beings. It's just, right now, ugh."

He carried them to their playpen. They weren't happy about it, but he needed a plan.

He called Kylie. He only needed advice, not help. For whatever reason, he wanted to be able to do this on his own. Maybe to prove to himself that this was one more thing he was capable of doing.

He could clean up and dress the twins. He could fix them bottles of watered-down ginger ale, he could feed them a cracker. They would survive and so would he.

And it didn't hurt that he would be Daisy's hero. Shouldn't he get hero status for taking care of two sick babies?

Daisy woke up in her bed, the curtains drawn and a blanket pulled up over her. She started to move, but the motion made her stomach heave. She put a hand to her head and waited for the sickness to pass. Rolling to her side, she saw a note on the nightstand, and next to it, a package of saltine crackers and a glass of water. She sat up to take a drink, then reached for the note. The writing was harsh and haphazard. She thought about how difficult it must have been to go from right-handed to left.

Daisy,
The girls are fine. They no longer smell. I
found clean clothes for them and got them
to eat crackers. We're here if you need us,
just ring the bell.
Joe

She saw the bell on the bed next to her pillow. He'd covered her, brought her something
to drink and eat, a bell and the sweetest, yet
most unromantic note, ever. She folded the piece
of paper and slid it under her lamp where it
wouldn't be lost.

After nibbling on the crackers, she curled up
under the soft throw blanket and realized he'd
managed to find things in the moving boxes that
had been delivered the previous day.

As she closed her eyes she grinned, thinking
that it was nice to know she wasn't alone.

When she woke up again, her room had gone
from bright, filtered light to dark and hazy. She
glanced at the window and saw a glimpse of
gray and scarlet as the sun shifted and sank on
the western horizon. She had to get up!

But she moved too quickly and her head
started to swim. For a few seconds, she remained where she was, eyes closed, breathing
deeply. She tried again and managed to make
it to the closed bedroom door.

Voices reached her. Male voices. She reached for the doorknob but paused. They were singing. A hymn, one she hadn't heard in years, drifted through the door. She realized there were several voices blending together. A quartet? Of men?

She glanced in the full-length mirror on the door and smoothed her hair into a more presentable ponytail before easing the door open and slipping out. She didn't want them to know she'd heard or that she was watching. Carefully she eased down the hall in the direction of her front sitting room.

At the entry she paused, listening to the group sing "Jesus Take My Hand," then she peeked. The men—there were four—had their backs to her. The twins were in their playpen watching, not fussing. They wore matching pink sleepers, and each girl had a tiny bow in her thin red curls. He'd unpacked more than one box, it seemed.

"Mama," Miriam cried.

The jig was up. Joe turned and spotted her.

"You're up. I hope we didn't wake you."

"You didn't. But I didn't expect a concert."

The other guys began to gather up instruments and music books. "We were just going," one of them said.

"I'm late for dinner," said another.

They were nervous. She was amused by the reaction.

"You don't have to go," she said. "I can take the twins to the other room."

"No, don't take the twins," a ruddy-faced older man told her. "They're the best audience we've ever had. They didn't yawn or laugh."

"We were just finishing up," Joe explained. He reached into the playpen for Myra and handed her to Daisy. "I managed to keep them safe."

"Thank you." She somehow got the words out but her heart was hammering, and suddenly the room seemed too small for all of the people gathered. It seemed too small because Joe was so close, his concerned gaze traveling over her face.

The men started to gather their instruments. Daisy moved out of their way, situating Myra on her left so she could pick up Miriam. Joe gave her another thoughtful, tender look. It was a look she didn't deserve from him.

The men left with Joe following them out, helping to carry their sound equipment. Daisy sat on the sofa, with the twins cuddled close. Joe returned, looking a little sheepish.

"We practice on Tuesday nights. I didn't want to leave you so I invited them here."

"I don't mind," she told him. "Honestly. You all sounded amazing."

"Thank you. It's something we started this past summer. We enjoy it a lot, and we're singing for the Christmas fundraiser pie auction."

"I see." She studied the babies in her arms. "These two are very clean. You did this yourself."

A hint of red colored his cheeks. "I have to confess, I called Kylie for help. She bathed them and changed them. Do you think I could do bows in hair?"

"I think you can do anything," she said. Her face grew hot at the words.

"Wait until you see the things I actually did before you make up your mind about that," he said with a wink. "I might have unpacked some of your boxes."

"You really didn't have to do that."

He shrugged off her objection. "It seemed the best thing to do while the twins napped. You'll find your kitchen organized and tidy, a pot of chicken soup is cooking and there's a surprise on the front porch."

"Chicken soup?"

"My grandmother's recipe."

"Did you talk her into coming over and cooking while Kylie bathed the babies?" she teased.

"No, I called her and got the recipe. I happen

to be a very good cook. I'm thirty-three years old, Daisy. If I didn't cook, I'd starve or be at a restaurant every meal. Come on, I have to show you something. But you might want boots and a blanket to wrap around you."

He reached for Myra and the little girl went happily, clinging to him as he picked up a throw blanket from the couch to wrap around her. Where had all of these blankets come from?

Rather than think about how he'd made himself at home, cooking chicken soup and unpacking her stuff, she went to her room where she slipped her feet into fuzzy slippers and grabbed the throw blanket off her bed to wrap around herself and Miriam.

Joe waited for her at the front door.

"Step outside and then close your eyes."

She did as she was told, then he counted to three.

"Open your eyes," he commanded.

Her porch and windows were lit up with twinkling, multicolored Christmas lights. The shrubs at the corners of the porch were covered in lights as well, and the outline of a manger sat off to one side. The babies giggled at the sight.

"How…how did you do all this?"

"Kylie watched the girls while I ran to the feed store. They have everything, you know.

And then the guys came by for practice and we did this before we started singing."

"This is quite possibly the kindest thing anyone has ever done for me," she told him. Emotion made her throat tight. She didn't want to cry. She didn't want him to look at her with sympathy. Instead, she wanted to stand there in her yard and enjoy this moment of homecoming, of having people who cared, people who would make something like this possible.

She leaned her head against his shoulder as she looked at the lights twinkling against the backdrop of the dark midnight blue of a winter sky.

"We should get you and the twins back inside where it's warm."

As they walked through the house to the kitchen, greeted by the savory aroma of chicken soup, a thought popped into her head that she didn't much like.

"What?" Joe asked as he settled Myra in her high chair.

"Nothing."

"That is not a nothing look," he said as he pulled bowls from the cabinet.

She placed Miriam in the second high chair and watched as Joe ladled soup into two adult-sized bowls and two baby bowls. He deserved the truth. She was a person who didn't easily trust or let go of suspicions. Thanks to her ex-husband, she always wondered about motivations. If someone was kind, if they helped her, if they acted too concerned, red flags popped up for her. She didn't want to be that person.

"Are you doing all of this because I'm helping you?" she finally asked.

He set the ladle on a plate and turned to look at her, his left arm holding his right elbow. He stood for a minute and then he crossed the room to where she stood.

"Are you limping?" she asked him, focusing on that rather than her own foolish thoughts.

"A horse stepped on my foot. It was your brother's fault. He was warning me off. Here's what happens to Joe if Joe hurts Daisy. I have no intention of hurting you, by the way. And I'm here because I'm your friend, not because I owe you. I'm pretty insulted that you think I'm that person."

"But I forced you," she said, trying to explain. "I told you I'd be the pretend fiancée if you'd hang Christmas lights."

"Christmas lights, Daisy. Not stinky babies, exposure to a stomach bug and my grandmother's chicken soup. To be honest, I'm not even sure why I'm here."

"Because you always seem to show up when

I'm at my worst." She touched his arm and he flinched, pulling away from her.

"Don't," he warned. "I'm not a little boy who needs your sympathy. I'm a grown man who knows my own mind. I'm not sure why I keep showing up when you need someone, but I think it's time that you realize there are men in the world who don't hurt women. There are decent men who will drive a woman home and treat her with respect. Women ought to want a man like that. They should realize their value and expect to be treated like someone who is valued. Value yourself, Daisy. Don't expect less because some men treated you as less."

He headed for the door and she wanted to go after him, but she had Myra and Miriam, and she didn't know how to apologize to possibly one of the most decent men she'd ever known.

He deserved far more than a fake fiancée who didn't know how to trust.

Chapter Seven

By seven o'clock Thursday morning, Daisy had realized a few truths. First, being a mom was hard work. She'd known about that one since she started caring for the girls, but it had grown more apparent over the course of the virus. Second, she was so sleep-deprived she couldn't think straight. And third, her back hurt from walking the floor with twins all night.

Fortunately, Kylie, Rebecca and even Sierra had been on hand to help the previous day. And Holly had sent Colt to the house with food.

Unfortunately, today was too busy to rest. She was due in court at eleven, then Lindsey would have a supervised visit with the girls. The day would be long, tiring and emotionally draining.

The twins were sleeping so she made good use of her time, preparing what they would need for the day, getting herself ready and starting a pot of coffee.

As she poured her first cup, the dog, which she now called Piper, ran to the front door and started to turn in circles. Daisy peeked out the window and groaned. Joe's truck had pulled up out front. The dog had obviously formed an attachment to the cowboy. Joe had managed to charm everyone in her life. Everyone but her. And if for some reason she actually was charmed, she didn't want to admit it.

She opened the door and put a finger to her lips. The twins were sleeping in the nursery off her bedroom. She doubted they would hear him, but she didn't want to take any chances.

Joe hurried up the steps to the porch carrying a plate covered with plastic wrap. He wore an unsure smile. She immediately worried she'd ruined what had felt like the beginning of a friendship. But then, she seemed to derail relationships wherever she went.

"What are you doing here?" she asked. As soon as the words left her mouth, she realized she needed a do-over. "I mean, hi, Joe. I'm surprised to see you. Come in and have some coffee. It's 7:00 a.m., but whatever."

He chuckled. "I'm here because you have a court date today, and I told you I would be there to represent Lindsey. The problem is, I'm not able to. I have a conflict of interest."

"You do?"

He nodded. "I do. I can't represent the twins' mother because I know and care about them. If she shares anything or does anything contrary to their best interests, I won't be able to give her the wise counsel she's entitled to."

"I see. That's bad, isn't it?"

"It could be, but I brought cinnamon rolls from Maria, which always makes me feel better. Also, I made some calls yesterday and found Lindsey a new lawyer." Once again, he had gone above and beyond. She placed her hand on his smoothly shaved cheek. His cologne, a subtle scent that was masculine and outdoorsy, wafted up to her nose. It was the kind of greeting that made her take an abrupt step back as soon as it happened.

"Thank you for the cinnamon rolls," she blurted out as she reached for the plate. "Tell Maria I said thank you."

"Are you telling me to leave?"

"Well, you clearly no longer have to go with us. You took care of the problem and Lindsey has an attorney."

"I'm still going with you, Daisy," he informed her. "If you want."

If she wanted. He'd effectively put the ball in

her court. She stood there a moment, a plate of cinnamon rolls in hand and a handsome cowboy on her front porch offering to do what? Be her support system?

All of a sudden, she became aware of the cold. "We should go in."

"Good idea."

She headed for the kitchen, knowing he'd follow. "Would you like a coffee."

"So, I can stay?" He sounded amused rather than confused.

"You can stay," she told him. Coffee and cinnamon rolls would make everything better. "But I have to leave by eight."

"I'm going with you," he repeated, then took the cup of coffee she offered and sat down at the butcher block table in the center of her kitchen.

Daisy turned up the baby monitor and watched the screen. She smiled at the sight of the twins cuddled together in their crib. The dog had left the kitchen and Daisy wasn't surprised to see the animal sneak into the bedroom with them. For a moment she watched the babies, then she gave a sigh and sprawled on the floor next to their crib.

"That dog has adopted you all as her family," Joe said softly.

"Yes, she has. I'm glad she found us." She poured her coffee and carried it to the table.

Sitting across from Joe, she thought that maybe she should also be glad this man had found her.

Joe got up and found plates, forks and napkins. He knew where to find those things; he'd unpacked them for her.

"Don't mind me," he told her. "I haven't had breakfast. I told Maria we had to leave early, and she thought we should have something to eat."

"That's kind of her. No, it was more than kind. I'm glad she's a part of our family."

"I think everyone feels that way."

She took a bite of a cinnamon roll. After a minute she worked up the courage to say what had been on her mind. "About the other night. I want to apologize. I…"

"Stop." He raised his left hand. "I really understand and I want us to go forward. There's no reason for us to keep going backward."

"That makes it sound like a relationship, and this isn't a relationship."

He studied her for a moment. "It isn't a relationship and yet, it is. It's at least a friendship."

A small cry on the monitor alerted them to the twins stirring in their bed. She glanced at the screen, while shoving a bite of cinnamon roll in her mouth.

"I have to get them ready to go."

"Can I help?"

"I've got this. Their bag is packed. I'll get them dressed and fed and then we'll head out. Oh wait, my chickens need to be fed."

"Chickens?" He looked lost.

"They were delivered yesterday."

"Not in the moving van, I hope!" he joked, already headed for the back door.

"No, I bought them from a local farmer. He delivered them yesterday, fixed up the chicken coop in the backyard for me, and then the feed store delivered feed."

"Chickens," he muttered as he headed out the door.

His grumbling made her smile. His mere presence made her smile.

Three hours later, Daisy realized the difference it made having Joe at her side. He'd helped them get out of the house on time and then he'd offered to drive. But all of that paled in comparison to having him with her as they walked into the courtroom where Lindsey already waited, her new attorney at her side. Lindsey immediately stood as she wiped away tears. She silently mouthed that she loved her babies, then her attorney told her to sit back down.

The next fifteen minutes of the proceeding went exactly the same as every other court date they'd had since the twins had been taken into protective custody. They discussed progress made, ground lost, Lindsey's new job, her housing situation, and the items on her case plan that still need to be completed. And then they discussed the latest drug test.

Daisy held Myra and Joe held Miriam as the judge listened to the information. He finally looked at Lindsey and the gloom that overtook the room was palpable.

"Miss Nolan, do you understand the severity of what you've done? You took more than six months of good behavior and set yourself back at least six months. Do you understand the importance of maintaining your sobriety and staying clean? Do you understand that the relationships you form are going to affect the decisions you make? You were a college student with a promising future. You have the opportunity to get that person back or lose her forever."

"Your honor, I am trying. I want my babies, I do. I want to visit them. I want to see them on holidays."

"I do not doubt your honesty, Miss Nolan. What I doubt is your determination to do what is best for them."

"Can I still see them today?" Lindsey asked as she glanced over at them.

"With supervision, yes. I'll set a new court date. And as soon as today's visit is completed, you will take another drug test."

"But I have to be somewhere."

"Nowhere you have to be is as important as this, Miss Nolan. And your reluctance to comply causes me to doubt your ability to pass this test. Good day, Miss Nolan."

Lindsey left the courtroom with her lawyer. The caseworker followed. Daisy, Joe and the twins walked out behind them. They met the caseworker waiting for them in the corridor.

"We'll let her meet with the twins. I have a room downstairs that's vacant. If you want to go with me, we'll meet her down there. Your friend can wait on the benches in the hallway."

They followed the caseworker down a flight of stairs and through a maze of hallways to a meeting room where Lindsey waited. The caseworker took Miriam and pointed toward a set of benches on a far wall.

"It'll be okay," Joe whispered close to Daisy's ear, then he kissed her cheek. "Hang in there, mama bear."

Mama bear. The name nearly undid her. Or maybe it was the sweetest kiss ever and the way he made her not quite so alone. Daisy smiled up at him, gave him a quick nod and with Myra in her arms, entered the room where Lindsey waited.

Lindsey looked up from studying her fingernails, nails that used to be perfectly neat and polished. It hit Daisy that this woman was not the same person who had worked in Daisy's store as an assistant. This woman had sunken cheeks and hopeless eyes. But those eyes lit up when she saw her daughters.

Lindsey got up to greet them, going first to the caseworker and Miriam.

"Oh Myra, my sweet baby. I've missed you." She reached for Miriam and the little girl pulled back.

"That's Miriam," Daisy told her. "Here's Myra. She has the yellow ribbon in her hair."

She handed the baby to her mother, knowing that Myra would be the twin more willing to go to this woman who was really a stranger to them. The twins had been in Daisy's care for almost ten months, practically their whole lives.

"They're getting so big." Lindsey kissed Myra's cheeks and carried her to a rug on the floor where she sank down to play with her daughter.

Daisy sat next to her, placing Miriam close to her twin to ease the transition to Lindsey. They played for a while and Lindsey cuddled both girls. She sang to them and told them stories about her own mother and how she'd been a single mom, too.

"If she was here, she'd make sure we were all okay," Lindsey told the twins. "I would have been better if she had stayed."

If she had stayed. Daisy's heart broke. Lindsey's mother had taken her own life several years ago.

"You'll be okay," Daisy said encouragingly. "The girls need you to be okay, Lindsey."

"I know they do," Lindsey shot back. "I don't need for you to tell me what my daughters need. They're mine, Daisy, not yours."

"I know that, Lindsey."

"I'm sorry." Lindsey reached for Daisy's hand. "It isn't your fault. I know that. I just… sometimes I get so frustrated and I think of them with you. And I know they love you and think you're their mom. They don't even know me. I'm just a stranger."

"It doesn't have to be that way," Cheryl, the caseworker, interjected, moving closer to the four of them. "Lindsey, you have to make better choices for yourself and your daughters. You could have had overnight visits. Now we have to wait longer."

"I'm aware of that. But I'm going to do this. I'm going to make it and get my girls back." Lindsey stood suddenly, upsetting Myra who had hold of her knee. The little girl fell back, crying as she tumbled. "I'm sorry. I didn't mean to do that."

"I know you didn't," Daisy assured her as she lifted Myra and soothed her.

"We'll have to end the visit in a few minutes," Cheryl informed them.

"But we haven't had a long enough visit. I need more time with my girls." Lindsey reached for Miriam, holding her close, even as the little girl cried.

There was nothing good about this situation. Daisy felt sick and her heart ached as Lindsey fell apart, wanting things to be right and not knowing how to make it right.

Cheryl approached them, sinking to her knees next to the distraught mother. She carefully removed Miriam from her arms and handed the baby to Daisy.

"Lindsey, you have to leave this room with me. We need to do the drug test now. If you don't, you'll set yourself back even further."

Lindsey kissed Myra's head. "I'm sorry, baby girl. I didn't mean to hurt you." Then she rushed out the door.

Daisy remained on the floor with both twins, now tired and resting their heads against her shoulders. Lindsey had turned into a person she no longer recognized.

Cheryl apologized. "I'm not sure what to say or what's going to happen. We'll have another court date soon."

Then she left and Daisy remained on the

floor, the twins cuddled close. She knew she needed to get up. But she needed a moment.

The door opened again, and there stood Joe, tall and solid. She blinked away the tears flooding her eyes, but she couldn't hold them back for long. When he crossed the room and pulled her and the twins close, the dam burst and she cried until her eyes were dry.

Joe held Daisy—who had unexpectedly fallen apart—in his arms. After several minutes she finally regained control and pulled away from him. He didn't have a handkerchief, so he searched the room and spotted a box of tissues. He set the box on a nearby table and took Myra from her.

"I take it the visit didn't go well?" he asked as he took a seat.

Daisy wiped her eyes and sat next to him with Miriam.

"I don't know her. I thought I did, but this woman is not the woman who used to work for me."

"Drugs change people. She might never again be the person you knew."

"Then what?" she said, her meaning obvious. The twins.

"Are you ready to be a mother to these little

girls?" he asked. "Are you prepared for it to be permanent?"

"I don't really know," she said, kissing the top of Miriam's head. "I love them. When I took them, it was meant to be six months. It's turned out to be a bit longer than that. I really thought Lindsey would pull herself together."

"What are you willing to do if she doesn't get it together? Ever?"

Closing her eyes, she pulled Miriam close. He thought perhaps she was praying so he remained quiet, giving her time. And he prayed for them himself. He prayed for Daisy and the twins. He prayed for Lindsey. He prayed for himself, because he was getting in deeper than he'd expected, and didn't know what God meant for him to do in this situation.

"I don't know," she finally answered. "I don't know if I'm the right person to raise them. What if there is a family out there that would be better for them? A mom, a dad, maybe some siblings?"

"What if a family for these twins is a mom who would do anything for them? This decision, that's between you and God. I can't give you answers."

She looked up. "So, the God I've ignored for most of my adult life because I didn't see too much of His intervention in my teen years when

I pleaded for His help, is now the God who is going to guide me in this situation?"

"I'm sorry," he told her, leaning close because he couldn't put his arm around her.

She took matters into her own hands. She shifted Miriam to her right side and with her left hand she reached for his right arm and moved it around her shoulder.

The moment took him by surprise, but it felt like the sweetest gift ever. His right arm was around her back and she remained close to his side.

"I don't know how to tell you to trust, Daisy. I've been there, wondering how I was supposed to give my anger, my fear over to a God who had allowed this—" he gave a sideways look at his arm "—to happen to me. In the hospital I was told to pray, to trust God, that He had a plan. Trusting God was the furthest thing from my mind. But the seeds were planted. One day, when I hit bottom and had nowhere else to go with my anger, I went to the hospital chapel and I yelled at Him. I gave Him every bit of my anger, my frustration and my fear and then I asked Him for help because I couldn't do it on my own."

"And your life has been perfect ever since?"

"No, it sure hasn't. It's been rocky. There are good days and bad. There are plenty of tough moments. But through it all, I've leaned on a source of strength that has helped me find peace and joy, even in the most difficult times. I've learned to be content no matter what my situation. That contentment comes from a deeper source than my own strength or power to change my life."

"I get it, Joe, I really do. And I want it. I want it the same way I want a relationship with my dad and my brothers. But being able to trust them to not let me down… That's the sticky part."

"Give it time."

She remained silent for a moment. "We should go," she finally said.

"We should. I want you to know I'm going to be here for you. I consider you a friend, Daisy. Whatever you and the girls need, I'm here."

"Can you repair a hot water heater?" she asked in a teasing voice.

"I can call an electrician," he answered. "Or a plumber. I'm very good at calling the right professionals."

"You're a keeper, Joe Lawson."

"Good to know because about ten minutes ago I got a text from my mother asking us to join them for dinner some time."

She groaned. "All of this sweet friendship stuff was just to butter me up?"

She started gathering up baby stuff. He watched, impressed by her ability to hold Miriam, while picking up toys, gathering cups and treats.

"I'm all about trying to butter you up," he told her.

She hung the baby bag over his right shoulder. "And I'm all about taking advantage of your kindness and strength."

"Then we're even."

"Almost."

They walked out of the building and headed to the parking lot where they'd left his truck. Across the street he spotted Lindsey watching. She waved, then turned and walked away.

They left Tulsa in early afternoon traffic. The girls were jabbering to each other in the back seat, and the radio played a country song about taking a guy home to meet the parents. Daisy kept her face turned toward the passing scenery out the window and their conversation had remained stilted. No, she wasn't hungry. The babies had eaten a snack while visiting their mother and they'd had a bottle.

When the jabbering ended, he glanced in the rearview mirror. The twins were both asleep. The day hadn't really interfered with their lives much. Daisy had taken the brunt of the day's emotions.

A sign on the side of the road advertised Christmas trees. Four miles ahead. He continued to watch for signs, and when he reached the road, he slowed and turned right. Daisy looked his way. "Where are we going?"

He pointed with his right arm. "The outside of your house is decorated for Christmas, but you still need a tree."

"You don't have to," she told him.

"We're already here." He parked his truck in the lot where trees of all sizes waited to be bought. "And these trees can be planted in the yard after Christmas. Imagine, your own forest of Christmas trees. When the twins are older, you'll have one for each Christmas. Think of the memories."

"The twins will be with their mother by then," she stated as she got out of the truck and unbuckled Myra.

He couldn't help her unbuckle or buckle car seats. That was a definite source of frustration for him. He had to wait for her to do it. When she handed Myra to him, her gaze caught and held his.

"The twins will go home," she told him. "That's the way it's been planned from the beginning. And I don't know what I'll do when that happens. But I also can't imagine the heartbreak of keeping them and knowing how much

Lindsey will miss them and want them. Either way, there'll be heartbreak at the end of this journey. I did this thinking I would be doing a good and happy thing for a friend. There is nothing about this that feels good or happy."

"Not right now, no, but hopefully someday it will be a better memory." He brushed hair back from her face with his right elbow. She didn't flinch.

She ripped his heart right out of his chest by closing her eyes and leaning into his touch. Acceptance could undo a man faster than anything.

With a sigh she opened her eyes and headed toward the rows of trees, and he followed.

"I'm not sure where I'm putting this tree in the house, so I'm not sure how big it should be," she told him.

"Why not two trees?" he suggested.

"One for my sitting room and one for the family room by the kitchen. I like that idea. I hope the twins aren't allergic to evergreens."

"That would be bad," he agreed. He surveyed the dozens of trees. They came in all sizes.

They walked side by side, each carrying a twin. Myra jabbered and pointed in her typical outgoing way. Miriam leaned into Daisy and took it all in with those big blue eyes of hers. She did raise her head at one point to watch when a bird swooped around them, then landed on a nearby tree.

"We can't take that one, sweetie," Daisy said. "I bet she has a nest in there."

She walked a few more feet and stopped in front of a tree that stood a foot taller than Joe. Next to it was a smaller tree. She walked around both, talking to herself and eyeing those trees up and down, peeking into the branches. He guessed she wanted to make sure there were no living creatures that could be brought into her home.

"What do you think?" he finally asked.

"These two. Definitely," she told him.

He waved at the farmer who had set up the tree lot and pointed at the two trees they would take, asking if someone could load them into his truck. Before Joe could pay, Daisy pulled out her purse.

"I'm paying for my own trees, Lawson."

"But I wanted to do this for you and the twins," he argued.

She ignored him and paid the tree guy. "Don't worry, I'll let you carry them into the house. I'll even let you help decorate. But I'm paying for my own trees, cowboy."

With cheeks rosy from the walk and the cool air, she turned to him, smiling. Her silvery eyes were full of light and laughter, and Myra had pulled off the blue knit cap she wore so that her dark hair blew around her face. She was the most beautiful woman he'd ever known.

He leaned in close, because he couldn't see wasting this moment. There might not be mistletoe but this moment was meant for kissing. She must have known because she looked up, her eyes shifting from silver to smoke. He edged closer, close enough that his lips touched hers. Then Miriam lifted his hat from his head and Myra started to cry.

He stepped back, laughing, aware of Daisy's presence and the joy that danced in her eyes.

"If you're paying, I'm going inside to buy a few decorations. I want to be a part of your Christmas with these girls, Daisy. I want to see them smile when the lights go on the trees and I want to watch them try to unwrap the gifts and pull off the ornaments."

"You want a lot, Joe." Her voice grew soft, troubled.

"I know. It didn't start out that way. But when a man is gifted with a fiancée and two little girls, it makes him wonder what else is missing from his life."

"It isn't real, remember?" she whispered.

"I know, but for a little while, let's pretend." He thought back to what she'd said about the twins. No matter how this played out, at the end of the journey, there would be heartache. Guaranteed.

Chapter Eight

Daisy spent Friday unpacking the rest of her boxes and settling into her new home. She'd been back for a week, and it seemed that every day there were things besides unpacking that filled her time. She wanted her new house to feel like a home, and that meant putting things away and decorating. She did love to decorate. She hoped, in time, she could build an interior decorating business, maybe even have a store in Hope.

As she moved through the house, she tried to ignore the Christmas trees that Joe had carried in the previous afternoon. They were undecorated, and he'd promised to come back and help. That meant another day in his presence. She didn't know how much more her heart could take of his "presence."

With the dog at her side and the baby monitor

clipped to the waist of her pants, she climbed the wide staircase upstairs. There were four large bedrooms, a smaller bedroom and two bathrooms on the second floor of her new home. She thought the smaller bedroom would be a nice library–sitting room. The other rooms were decorated and waiting for inhabitants.

Faith House was now more than a dream. It was on the cusp of being reality. In this house she would provide a new beginning for abused women and their children. She would help them find jobs, gain independence and hopefully learn to believe in themselves. Her experience with abuse was that it stole that part of a woman that helped her feel strong. The more she was beat down, the more she started to feel that she deserved the abuse.

No one deserved to be abused.

Daisy knew because she'd been there. She'd been her husband's victim from "I do" until the night she called 911. Self-consciously she tugged at her scarf, wishing she didn't have these memories. Wishing she could take off the scarf and tell the world the abuse, the scar—none of it mattered. He'd tried to steal her self-worth, her independence and then her life. He hadn't succeeded.

She was a survivor. There were times she had to remind herself of that fact.

This house would give other women the opportunity to find themselves again. They would learn to be survivors and not victims. She stood there, dreaming about how this would all look when her reverie was interrupted by a knock on the front door. She peeked out the upstairs bedroom window and recognized the SUV parked in her circle drive. Her brother Carson.

He knocked again. She ran down the stairs as quietly as she could. Opening the front door, she whispered, "Babies. Napping."

"Oops, sorry. I thought I'd come by for coffee."

"I'm busy unpacking."

He didn't seem bothered by that. Instead, he followed her inside. "Then I'll help you unpack."

"No, I'll make some coffee." When they got to the kitchen, she checked the monitor that showed twin babies sleeping soundly in their crib.

"They're pretty awesome," Carson told her as he poured himself a cup of coffee.

"They are. I'm not sure what I'll do when they go back to Lindsey."

"Back?"

"To their mother. The goal is still reunification. I told her I'd help make that happen. I'm not going back on my promise."

"I know you're not. But it won't be easy, letting them go."

"No, it won't be easy." It would break her heart. That much was true.

They sat together in the family room, each with a cup of coffee they weren't drinking and with a plate of cookies on the table. The dog looked at the cookies and whined until Carson tossed one to her. Piper snapped up the cookie and then licked her lips, waiting for another.

"What's his name?" Carson asked.

"He is a she and her name is Piper. I think she's probably going to have puppies."

Carson smiled at that. "You named her after our collie."

"I missed that dog," she admitted.

"I missed you," Carson told her. "Every day, I've missed you. And I've wondered what it was we did that made you push us all away. I would have been there for you. You were there for me."

When his wife was killed in a tragic accident, nine months pregnant with his daughter, Maggie. The baby had survived. Daisy had stayed with his son while he'd been at the hospital with his baby girl.

"Yes, I was there for you." She reached for a cookie and rather than taking a bite, she held it out to the dog.

"Then why?"

"I don't trust you."

He sat in stunned silence for a moment. "What does that mean?"

"You weren't there, Carson. When I needed you, you either didn't notice or you were gone. You had no idea how much I needed you."

"I didn't know that your husband was abusive."

"Bill, Carson, not my husband. Our stepfather."

"Bill?" He stumbled over the word. "He hurt us all."

"He hurt me in ways he didn't hurt you. He hit you. He beat Colt. He did more to me. And you weren't there." She fought the sting of tears, drawing in a deep breath as her throat tightened.

This was not the conversation she wanted to have with him.

He got up and walked to the back door. His hand hit the door frame, anger causing his shoulders to tense.

"I'm so sorry. I should have noticed. I should have done something. Forgive me." He finally turned to face her again, and she hated that he wouldn't look at her.

"I'm working on that." She got the words out, and she meant them. "And really, I know it isn't fair to blame you, but I have. I'm working on that."

"I always thought you were the strong one, the happy one."

She laughed, the sound harsh. "It felt better, pretending that nothing was wrong and that I had it all together. It was easier to be the fun-loving and mischievous Daisy. I laughed, I smiled, I put on my makeup and I conquered the world. You all thought I was crazy and adventurous. I was just hiding how angry I felt… and how small."

He returned to the small sofa and sat across from her. The table between them. A chasm filled with heartache and grief separating them.

"I wish I could go back," he eventually said. This time he looked at her. Their gazes locked and held.

"I don't want to go back," she told him. "Going back would mean reliving those days. I'm only interested in moving forward."

Just then, she heard the twins begin to cry on the monitor she'd set next to her.

"I have to get them," she told him.

"I'll help."

Together, they went to get the twins from the crib. The room was shadowy in the late afternoon light. Carson picked up the twin standing at the side of the crib. "Is this Myra?"

"It is."

"How do you tell them apart?"

She smiled at the little girl she'd lifted from the bed. The twin with the darker curl that grew at the nape of her neck. Her eyes were just a shade lighter blue. "This is Miriam. Notice her eyes."

"I see it. Her eyes are a winter sky."

"Aren't you poetic," she teased. "This is how you got Kylie back after all of those years."

"Yes, poetry and charm."

They stood on opposite sides of the crib, silent. Finally she sighed. "I'm home because I want to fix our relationship. I want my family, my brothers and my father. I want to build a family."

"And fill this house with children?" he asked.

"No, this is a home for women in need of a second chance. Faith House. And before you get all emotional, Faith was a friend of mine who lost her battle to escape her abusive husband."

They walked back through the house to the family room. The plate of cookies, now empty, was on the floor. She looked over at the dog curled up on a rug, innocent and happy.

"I'm glad you came home, Daisy. And if we can help with Faith House, we'd like to."

"I appreciate that." She glanced at the clock. "I have to go to the church and pick up Dixie. She's spending the weekend with us."

"I'm sure she's looking forward to that. You're her hero."

"She's young, she'll grow out of that," Daisy told him.

"I hope she doesn't. You're someone to look up to."

She hugged her brother, their first genuine hug in a very long time. She found that the more she shared her fear, her anger and distrust, the stronger she grew, and the more those old feelings faded away.

"You're someone to look up to, too," she told him.

They left the house together. He helped her put the twins in their car seats and told her he'd probably see her later at the church. They were decorating and preparing for the fundraiser that would take place Sunday evening. There would be food, music and a pie auction. It was the last fundraiser before the community Christmas dinner.

He'd told her all of this so that she would attend and be involved. Of course, she would be there. Dixie would be performing in the Christmas play during the dinner. She wouldn't miss that for the world.

When she walked into the church, she realized she might have been lured there under false pretenses. Dixie was still busy practicing for the play. There were several women, Rebecca and Kylie among them, who were decorating the fellowship hall and sanctuary.

"Finally, help has arrived." Rebecca called out.

"Help? Do I look like help?"

"Decorating?" Rebecca said, as if it were obvious.

Daisy looked at the gold ribbon her sister-in-law held. "What do you plan on doing with gold ribbon?"

"Swag it somewhere," Kylie told her. "Just make it look pretty."

"Do you have a better idea?" Rebecca asked.

Kylie laughed at that. "She's an interior decorator. She always has a better idea."

"I'm just here to pick up Dixie," she reminded her sister-in-law. She gave a pointed look to Myra on her left hip and Miriam on her right. "My hands are full."

"But Dixie can't leave yet, so you might as well help us. Come on, the nursery is open for small ones. The twins can play with the other children."

"I really should go," she said.

"It would do you and those little girls both some good to have a break." Kylie took Miriam. "They're with you all the time."

"Okay, I'll help." Daisy followed Kylie

through the church and they dropped the twins off at the nursery room, then they got down to decorating business.

"We need something other than gold ribbon," Daisy informed them.

"There are boxes of decorations." Kylie pointed to the tubs.

"We just knew that if you came in and caught us with the gold ribbon, you'd feel compelled to save us from our disastrous decorating." Rebecca didn't bother looking guilty.

Daisy couldn't help but laugh. "I've been played."

For the next hour they decorated, told stories and laughed. They finished the fellowship hall and moved on to the sanctuary. At the front of the room, Dixie and several other young people were singing "O Come All Ye Faithful." Daisy hummed along, remembering all the Christmas programs she'd attended as a kid.

"Sing with me," Kylie urged. "Remember when we were the angels that time?"

"We sang 'Silent Night,'" she said. She couldn't have been more than eight.

Kylie took hold of her hand and pulled her forward. "Girls, mind if we borrow Mrs. Pillar to play for us?"

Dixie grinned big. "Go for it."

"'Silent Night,'" Kylie called out to the pianist. She opened a hymnal and handed it to Daisy.

The pianist played the intro. Kylie began to sing and Daisy soon joined in. "Silent night, Holy night. All is calm. All is bright." The words brought a flicker of something that felt like hope.

The front doors of the church opened. Cold air rushed through the sanctuary. A man appeared in the dimly lit vestibule. He made his way forward, into the light, staying to the side of the room. She barely flicked a glance in his direction but she knew by his walk who it was. She knew him. She shouldn't feel that way about a man who was temporarily in her life. Should she?

As she sang, her gaze connected with his. Her heart yearned for more. More peace filling her heart. More joy that erased the pain of the past.

She yearned for more. But would she ever be brave enough to reach out and grasp it for herself?

Joe stood in the shadows near the door, listening to Daisy and Kylie sing "Silent Night." As they finished, he stepped forward. She caught his eye, and for a brief second, he thought she looked happy to see him. And in that moment, his world shifted, because he wanted her to be happy to see him.

"Sounds amazing, ladies," he called out, pulling off his cowboy hat as he approached them. "Will you sing it for the program?"

"I don't think so," Daisy said quickly.

"You should." He let it go. Pushing her wouldn't do any good. "I'm here to help you all with whatever needs doing."

"I think we've just about got it." Kylie grinned at him. "Good timing, showing up at the very end, Mr. Lawson."

While Kylie admonished him, he couldn't help but look at Daisy. Even in jeans and a sweatshirt, she rocked his world. "Actually, we had a sick cow and a horse with a foal we couldn't find."

"Did you find the horse?" Daisy asked.

"Yes, we did. She got out, we're not sure how, and managed to find herself up the road about a mile. They found her foal wandering along the fence."

"Do you think someone tried to steal the mare?" Kylie wanted to know. "There have been a lot of thefts reported around here."

"I think that's a good guess but I'm not sure how they got the mare away from the baby. Someone took Jerry Crawford's farm truck last week. Walked right into his barn and drove away with it."

"Jerry might have left it somewhere and got a ride home. He just doesn't remember," Colt added as he entered the sanctuary. "I didn't know about the truck, but I do know I saw him in an unmarked cop car about a week ago. Maybe Mrs. Crawford doesn't know what he's up to."

Rebecca shot her husband a warning look. "Gossiping in church, Isaac? Save that for the café."

"Ouch," Joe chuckled at the back and forth.

Dixie ran up to them. "The men told me to tell you all that dinner's ready. They're serving roast, potatoes, carrots and rolls."

"I got here just in time." Joe winked at Dixie. She laughed and headed off with her friends.

"Just in time to serve with the other men, you mean." Colt nodded toward the door. "See you ladies in a few. Joe and I have work to do."

Joe knew he couldn't get out of it, but he'd give almost anything to be able to hang back with Daisy. He really wanted to make her smile again. He wanted to watch the shadows drift from her silver-gray eyes. Unfortunately, Colt didn't plan on letting that happen. He was at the door, clearing his throat and jerking his head toward the fellowship hall.

If Joe cared to guess, he imagined Colt and the other West brothers were doing what they could to keep him away from their little sister. They all knew the engagement wasn't real. They had nothing to worry about. They definitely didn't need to concern themselves with him and his relationship with Daisy.

Joe followed Colt down the hall, not surprised at all when he stopped and refused to let him pass.

"I thought we were needed in the kitchen," Joe said as he tried to get past the other man.

"First we need to have a talk about my little sister."

"She's almost thirty years old," Joe reminded him.

"And still my sister. I don't want to see her hurt."

"You know that she started this, and that she's very capable of handling herself, right?"

"Yeah, I know all of that. It all started as a fun little game. Daisy and Joe and their fake engagement. Not very honest of you, my friend. Aside from that, you're spending a lot of unnecessary time with her and she's been hurt in the past."

"All things I'm very aware of." Joe pushed past Colt's arm. "I'm going to help serve now. This shouldn't come between us. We've been friends for a while. But I'm telling you to back off."

Colt stepped in front of him a second time. "Do you have feelings for my sister."

Joe couldn't believe he was having this conversation in the church hallway. "I might have feelings for your sister, but I also know that she's been hurt. She's trying to fix herself and thought that coming back to Hope would do the trick. But I know that it takes more than changing location to heal a person's past."

Colt leaned a shoulder against the wall. "Yeah, but I also know you're the guy who recently decided he wouldn't mind settling down. If God brought the right person along."

"Let it go," Joe warned. "She isn't interested in anything other than this fake engagement and friendship."

Colt put an arm around Joe's shoulders and together they started down the hall. "Then show her that a real relationship with a charming man such as yourself would be a lot better than a fake engagement."

"I don't think that's what she wants." Joe left it at that. They walked into the kitchen and saw the other men were filling cups with tea and fruit punch. A few were gloving up, preparing to serve. Someone pushed a pair of gloves into Joe's hand.

"Serve the rolls?" the older man asked.

"Will do." Because serving rolls meant steady

conversation with the people going through the line and blocking the thoughts Colt had evoked with all his questions and warnings.

The line moved quickly. He placed rolls on plates, chatted with the women as they walked through the food line and talked to the other men on the line about the price of cattle, the winter wheat and protecting their farms from the thieves that seemed to be circling like vultures. Normal, everyday conversations that mattered to the folks in Hope.

The best fishing spots. The price of gas. The price of hay for their livestock. No one mentioned Daisy, and for that he was thankful. He needed a minute to be the same old Joe he'd always been a little over a week ago.

She'd turned his life upside down and had him thinking crazy thoughts about the future.

As if he'd conjured her from thin air, Daisy was standing in front of him, her dark hair loose around her face and a shy expression that took him by surprise. He wondered if the shyness was the part most people missed, the way they never noticed that he wasn't as confident as he appeared. He'd never been confident. Not with women. He'd dated Cassidy because she'd been a family friend. He hadn't needed to approach her or ask her out ever. It had been planned for them since birth, if he had to guess.

"Roll?" he asked.

She grinned. "Please."

"Kiss?" he asked, knowing he shouldn't.

"Forget it," she said in a teasing voice. "I don't even know you. You're just some guy serving me dinner and now you want to kiss?"

He leaned a little. "People might think we like each other."

"We're engaged, aren't we? We should like each other a little."

"I do like you," he agreed.

He would have said more but late arrivals walking through the doors of the fellowship hall stopped him.

"What's wrong?" Daisy asked.

"Nothing," he said, but that wasn't the truth. "My family is here. I told them I was going to be here to help. I didn't think they'd show up, too."

"If I turn around, it'll be too obvious," Daisy said with a conspiratorial whisper. "Is Cassidy with them?"

"She is. And they're heading this way."

"Fun. I feel like we're a couple of teenagers about to get grounded."

Suddenly his grandmother and mother were upon them, smiling and chatting about wanting to help.

"My, doesn't this all look lovely?" his mother said.

"You should eat," Joe offered. "Plates are on the first table. As soon as we're finished serving the women and children, we men get to fill our plates."

"Oh, we've already eaten," his mother assured him.

"What is there for us to do?" his grandmother asked. "I would love to help."

Kylie approached, saving the day with her welcoming smile and ability to put everyone at ease.

"It's good to see you all. Why don't you at least have some dessert. We're going to start sorting gifts by ages and then into neutral, girls or boys. We also have to size coats and shoes. We would love the extra help. This is a massive undertaking and the more the merrier."

Daisy glanced his way and she winked. The wink floored him.

"We would love to help," Joe's mother assured Kylie. "And your father can do what he does best," Nana El said. "He can write a check."

Cassidy had moved to his side. Her smile didn't reach her eyes, but she seemed determined to pretend she was happy to be here. "Why don't you let me help serve food?"

"The men actually take responsibility for this meal," Kylie informed her with a smile. "But we'd love to have you help wrap gifts."

"Oh, of course." Cassidy continued to smile but the hardness in her pale blue eyes was difficult to miss. She turned to face Joe, shutting out the people around him. "I'm either here for us to get reacquainted or I'm not. But I'm not one for playing games."

Trying to hide his shock at her outburst, Joe rubbed his jaw.

"I guess you're not." He said it as simply as he could.

She stood there, frozen, her eyes bright with anger. He knew her well enough to know that she would hold it together. She wouldn't lose control. He also doubted she would let him off this easily.

He shrugged and went back to serving rolls.

Daisy gave him a sympathetic look as she moved on, filling her plate and leaving the kitchen to find a seat with Dixie and the rest of her family. He watched as his family and Cassidy moved on through the line.

He guessed he should feel bad for Cassidy. But he couldn't. He hadn't been the one to bring her here under false pretense; his parents and probably hers had.

His grandmother circled back around as his family moved to a table near the Wests.

"Nana El," he started.

She raised a hand to stop him. "I'm not going

to tell you what to do. I'm here to tell you that Cassidy is nervous and desperate. Her father was caught embezzling, and they're on the verge of financial destruction. That isn't your fault or hers. But she's a big girl. She's thirty-two, and her father's embarrassment isn't hers. She is well educated and can make a life for herself. She doesn't need you to clean up their tarnished reputation. You have a real chance at happiness here. I want you to take it."

"So do I." He leaned to kiss her cheek. "I love you, Nana."

"Back atcha, Joe. You never know, I might decide to stay and be an Okie. I like this little town of yours, and this church."

She hurried away, smiling big, greeting people and generally making friends wherever she went.

From across the room, he caught and held Daisy's gaze. Until her cheeks flushed pink and she turned away. For now, their pretend engagement served his purpose. It kept her in his life.

But how much longer could this go on? Joe didn't know.

Chapter Nine

On Saturday Joe met his parents for lunch at Holly's Café. He had to admit, he didn't mind having them in Hope. It proved to be the best of both worlds for him. He stayed in the town he had come to think of as his home, and he got to spend time with the people he cared about most. Even if it meant Cassidy sitting next to him, a possessive hand on his arm as she told him a long story about friends they'd grown up with and the successes they were enjoying.

Leena, the morning waitress, appeared at his side.

"Coffee?" she asked, her voice a little quieter than usual.

He glanced up at her and she looked away, but not before he saw the bruise on her cheek. Her lavender-streaked hair, normally in a ponytail, hung loose and fell forward to cover half her face. "Leena, you okay?"

"Of course I am," she told him with a big smile that didn't quite reach her eyes. "How about you, Joe? I heard you're marrying Daisy West. Congratulations."

"Thank you," he said, trying to avoid looking at his grandmother. "And yes, I'll take a refill."

She avoided eye contact as she refilled his cup, and then she hurried away. Next to him, Cassidy continued talking about every classmate she could think of. He didn't much care. He had kept in contact with some friends, but he didn't need a rundown of everyone he'd ever known since kindergarten.

The bell over the door clanged, and he glanced that way.

"You can stop looking. It isn't her." Cassidy poked at the salad she'd barely touched. "I'm here. And I've been a part of your life for thirty-one years."

"And you'll always be a good friend." He made eye contact with his father. "You should know, I'm buying property here. A few hundred acres, mostly grassland. I'm going to build a house and raise cattle. I'd like to show you."

"So you're going to be a rancher?" his dad asked. No condemnation, just a question.

"I'm also going to set up a small law office here. In Hope."

"I'd like to see the land, and the office." His dad pushed his plate back. "You've built a good life for yourself, son. I know I haven't always been supportive." He paused when Joe arched a brow at the understatement. "I've been the opposite of supportive. I'm glad we decided to stay longer and get better acquainted with your community. And your fiancée."

"However, we would like it if you would consider having a reception back in Connecticut," his mother told him. "After the wedding here. Whenever is convenient."

He rubbed the back of his neck as they went on, making plans and explaining how people at home would want to be a part of his happiness so it would be good for their family and friends who wouldn't be able to make the trip to Oklahoma. His grandmother caught his eye and wagged a finger at him. She was right; this was going too far.

"I'll discuss this all with Daisy." He cleared his throat as he glanced at his watch. "Speaking of Daisy, I have to go meet her. I'll see you all this evening at dinner."

"Do we need to bring anything for the fundraiser tomorrow? I can make a pie if you need me to," his mother said.

He stood as he answered. "The pies are made by the men in the church. Or that's what they want everyone to think. I have a feeling Holly, at the café, makes quite a few."

They all laughed.

"Wait for me, Joe." Nana El jumped up from her chair. "If you want that recipe, I have to make sure it's done well."

That stopped him in his tracks. He faced his spritely grandmother and wondered what she might be up to. "That wasn't part of the deal."

"I know it wasn't. I guess I'm a bit like my grandson. I'm not afraid to change course midstream."

"Is that what you're doing?" he asked. "What change of plans are we talking about?"

She took him by the arm and headed for the door. "You're going to make pies for the auction tomorrow, right? If you're baking my pie recipe, I'm going to help."

"But you weren't invited," he reminded her.

She laughed. "And neither were you, if I'm any good at guessing. We're both showing up unannounced and uninvited. But I'm very helpful and I love those baby girls."

"You're incorrigible."

"Yes, I am. Now let's go. I happen to have all of the ingredients in our car. You can thank me later for being better at planning these things than you'll ever be."

When they got to the truck, she had to stop a moment and catch her breath, but the gleam in her hazel eyes told him all he needed to know. She was having the time of her life.

"We need to get the groceries out of that monster vehicle your father rented. I don't know what it is about going to the country that makes a man think he needs a big truck. It isn't as if he's going off-roading."

"You never know. I'll get the groceries but you understand she might not want company?"

"Oh, leave that up to me. If you had to do this all on your own, you'd never get a wife."

"I can get a wife on my own, Nana El," he assured her.

"Can you get *this* wife?" she asked as she attempted to climb into his truck, complaining about vehicles that sat ten feet off the ground.

Joe hurried to help her. "Grab the handle," he pointed out. He put his arm around her and helped her make the step.

"Thank you, Joseph." She settled into the seat and he pulled out the seatbelt for her to pull around herself. He continued their earlier conversation.

"This wife, as you call her, is a woman who isn't interested in marriage. She told me I need someone who shares my faith. I wouldn't want to be unequally yoked, she said."

"For some reason, I don't think you're at all unequal. I think she's just in denial."

His grandmother was a smart woman.

"I think so, too," he admitted.

"How did this engagement come about? I think it surprised you as much as it surprised the rest of us."

Hard to believe it had been just over a week since Daisy sprang this on everyone. It seemed as if she'd always been in his life.

"Why do you think it isn't a real engagement?"

"I think we both know that I'm wise and all knowing. It comes with grandmother-hood."

He laughed but couldn't disagree.

"I think she thought she was rescuing me," he admitted. "And maybe a little of it was that she wanted to pay me back for being too nice."

"Can a man be too nice?" his grandmother asked.

"Maybe not, but I think we do get overlooked from time to time."

"It's a shame, really." His grandmother gave him a long look. "You're a good man. A man of faith. You'll make a good husband and father. I always prayed you would be this man. You had to take a long journey to get here."

He couldn't agree more. "Yes, it was a long journey and not always an easy one."

They pulled up to Daisy's house. He could see her in the backyard near the barn. She had the twins in a playpen, the dog lying next to it, protecting them. A gray horse, he guessed an Arabian, pranced around the field.

He parked and they headed for the back.

"This is a beautiful place," his grandmother said. "What in the world will she do with a house this size?"

"I'll let her share that with you," he answered as they walked toward the playpen. Dixie was nearby, blowing bubbles to keep the girls entertained. It was close to seventy degrees. A perfect day to be outside.

The dog growled a low warning as they approached. Joe called out to the animal and the growl changed to a whimper, her tail thumping a greeting. Daisy glanced back at them.

Joe left his grandmother with Dixie and the twins. She didn't seem to mind at all. She grabbed a nearby lawn chair and sat down. He closed the space between himself and Daisy, doing his best not to appear in too big a hurry to be at her side.

"What do you think of him?" she asked, referring to the horse. Her voice was bubbly and bright, as if it was Christmas morning and she'd gotten the toys she always wanted.

"He's nice," Joe told Daisy complimented as he stepped close to her side.

"Thank you. I've had him for a while, but he's been with a trainer on the other side of Tulsa. They just delivered him this morning." She whistled and the horse trotted to the fence. "You brought your grandmother?"

"I did. She invited herself, and she's not an easy woman to say no to."

"I imagine she's not. That leaves the other question, what are you doing here?"

"I'm here to get help bake pies for tomorrow. It's a nice engaged couple thing to do. Don't you think?"

"Except we aren't really engaged."

He reached for the horse, running his hand along the sleek, gray neck. "I should have asked first. I apologize."

"Not your fault. I think I'm just feeling cornered these days. I'm adjusting to my new life in the middle of my family and this fish bowl of a town. I'm trying to be the person everyone wants me to be, but I don't know who I am anymore."

"I think we all just want you to be you." He nudged his shoulder against hers. "I like the real you."

"The real me is a person who is still searching, not quite sure of who she is or what she believes. She is the exact opposite of the person you would really be in a relationship with."

That took him by surprise. "You're wrong. I think she's exactly the person I would be in a relationship with. She's honest and caring, and I think she has faith but she's trying to figure out how that faith fits into her life."

"Don't try to make this into something it isn't. You rescued me twice. I rescued you back. We're almost even."

Silence loomed between them. What could he say to that? Several options ran through his mind. He decided to pick one. "Hey, I'm just here to make a pie. My grandmother is going to help. By the way, she thinks you're perfect for me. But we can discuss that later."

"I'm holding you to that, cowboy."

"I understand. But my grandmother can be pretty determined. I think if you try to back out, she's going to double her efforts to see our wedding planned. She might order one of those online ordainment certificates so she can officiate herself."

That brought the humor back to her face.

"I do love your grandmother."

"Me, too. And she does make the best apple

pie I've ever had. But if this is really too much, I can make some excuse and we'll leave."

"I think I'm not letting you off that easily. I think Grandma should share some embarrassing baby Joe stories."

He groaned.

Daisy leaned across the fence to reach for the horse. She tossed a look at Joe. "You know too many of my stories. Time for me to know a few of yours."

His grandmother would tell stories. They would bake pies together. His heart would get a little more involved with a woman he considered remarkable, while she wanted nothing to do with a relationship.

He was in serious trouble.

"Why do the recipes tell us to mix the dough if that makes the crust less flaky?" Dixie asked Joe's grandmother.

Spry and energetic with short white hair that curled around her face and hazel eyes that matched her grandson's, Eloise popped an apple slice in her mouth, chewed a bit, then answered.

"That is a very good question. I think they must not make many pies if they think that's the way to make crust. The key to good flaky crust is not too much water and don't over mix. You stir just until it the ingredients all come together and then you ball it up and roll out half the dough for the bottom crust and half for the top. And if you have any leftover dough, you smear it with butter and sprinkle it with cinnamon and sugar and bake it."

"My mom," Dixie said. "I mean, Becky, who was my mom for a long time, she used to make pies but we never put cinnamon sugar on the crust."

"Well then, we'll start a new tradition." Eloise grabbed the first ball of dough and put it on a board that had been sprinkled with flour. "Let's roll this out and place it in the pie pan. Oh, we need to heat our pastries in the microwave. Joe, can you put those in for us?"

Joe was slicing apples that Daisy had peeled. He put the knife down and grabbed the plate of pastries, shoving them in the microwave and hitting the thirty-second button.

"While you all keep making the pies, I'll season the steaks for the grill. I might not be a baker, but I can grill a decent steak."

The oven buzzed as it heated and then it popped. Something that smelled suspiciously like burning wires filled the air and the kitchen went dark.

"I don't think that's supposed to happen," Dixie said as she glanced around the kitchen. "Are all of the lights out?"

"Is my house on fire?" Daisy asked. She looked to Joe.

"Don't panic. I think a breaker flipped. We must have overloaded it with all of the appliances. Let me take a look at the breaker box. Open a window and relax."

Daisy couldn't relax. She could only think of her beautiful house in ashes.

Joe touched her cheek, forcing her to look up at him. "Take a deep breath." He smiled as he said it.

Deep breath. She did as he asked, then went to open a window while he went in search of the breaker box.

"I think it's in the utility room," she called out as he headed in the wrong direction. "The other way."

A moment later he appeared with the phone in his hand. "Prairie Rose. Yeah, Daisy's house. Right."

"What are you doing?" Daisy asked?

Nana El ignored them. She was putting all of their pie ingredients in a bag, scooping sliced apples into containers and pie crust into storage bags. Daisy shot her a curious look.

"I called the fire department. The breaker was flipped, but I smell wires and smoke. I don't think you want to chance this. Why don't you go ahead and take the twins and Dixie outside? Nana El, that means you, too."

"Is the house on fire?" Daisy asked.

"Be calm," he advised.

"Yes, of course, be calm."

His calm didn't make sense. But she was grateful for it, because his calm was contagious. She packed a bag for the twins and for herself, then Nana El and Dixie helped her get everything outside to the backyard. It was still sunny and warm, so they moved the playpen to the shade of a nearby oak tree and waited.

It wasn't long before the blast of sirens filled the air. Daisy shuddered, thinking of the accident just a little more than a week ago. She thought of how it had felt to see Joe, knowing he was there to keep them safe.

She could get used to him being in her life, taking care of her. But then what? What happened when he let her down? When he hurt her?

He would never hurt her, not physically. She knew that. But he could hurt her in other ways.

"Where is Joe?" Nana El asked as they sat on a bench several feet away from the house. The sirens were near. No sign of smoke or fire.

"I'm going to find him. Please watch the twins." Daisy jumped up and hurried toward the house. She ran the last short distance.

As she ran through the door, she bumped into Joe. "Where were you!"

"Worried?"

She pounded her hand against his chest.

He covered her hand with his. "I was making sure the main breaker was off and checking the basement."

"You should have waited for the fire department."

He grinned at that, tipping his cowboy hat. "Ma'am, I *am* the fire department. Those sirens are just backup support."

"You're so full of yourself."

She was so near to tears she didn't want to talk to him. He seemed to sense that and his smile dissolved.

"I'm fine and I think your house is also fine. But there are some wiring issues. Being the helpful man I promised to be, I'll contact an electrician."

"I'm mad at you right now, so don't try to be charming."

"I can't help it. It's just who I am. Now, let's go outside. There is some smoke and I'm afraid a little damage to the wall in the utility room."

"This could have been bad."

"It could have been but it isn't. We were here, awake and not caught off guard."

The fire trucks had arrived and first responders swarmed her home. Joe led her back to the bench at the far side of the lawn, where his grandmother and Dixie waited with the twins. He picked up Myra, who giggled as he tickled her belly.

"I'm guessing you won't be able to stay here for a few days," Joe told Daisy. "You can go in to pack up some more things, but I wouldn't recommend taking the girls inside. The smell is pretty strong. It'll air out eventually, but it might not be what you want to breathe right now."

"I guess I can go to the resort."

Dixie pulled on her sleeve. "Stay with us."

"I don't think you all have room for us."

"We have an extra bedroom." Dixie's face lit up. "Or stay with Grandpa Jack."

Family or the resort. She looked longingly at her house, finally accepting that Joe had been correct. She couldn't stay here, not until the wiring issues were resolved and the house was aired out.

"I'll stay with my father at the ranch."

The words weren't easy to say, but she found the decision wasn't as difficult to accept as it might have been two weeks or even a week ago.

Two hours later, after making sure there were no hot spots, the fire department left. Joe had taken his grandmother to the rental house on the lake. Colt had come by to get Dixie and to sit with Daisy for a bit. Kylie and Carson had taken the twins to the ranch so they could get them fed and settled.

Daisy loaded her dog into the SUV she had rented, gave her home a last look and even said a prayer. She made the five-minute drive to Mercy Ranch with Piper sitting in the passenger seat next to her and the radio tuned to the country station.

When she parked at the back of the ranch house, Jack was waiting for her. He sat on the patio, a cup in his hand. He set the cup down and stood when he saw her. She got out, the dog jumping out after her. Her dad's favorite ranch dog, Mutt, ran over to give them an inspection and decide if the new kid could stay. The two dogs circled each other, growled, then with a sniff, decided to be friends.

She had no bags to get out of the car. Carson had taken care of everything. He was being the helpful, protective big brother, trying to earn her trust and forgiveness. Yes, warmth did trickle through her heart. She did want a relationship with all of the West men. She couldn't help the walls that she'd built, but maybe it was time to break down those walls and let people in.

"Rough day?" her dad asked as she joined him on the patio. He had a gas-fueled fire pit for warmth. They sat next to it and enjoyed the last vibrant rays of sunshine as evening settled in.

"Very. I'm exhausted."

"Maria told me to tell you to go get some sleep. She has the twins in her room, and she'll watch them through the night. She wants you to rest."

The offer brought a rush of tears she hadn't expected. She brushed them away. "That's very kind. She doesn't have to."

"She wants to. She loves those babies."

"I know. And she loves you, too."

"And I love her. It isn't a young man's love. We've grown to love each other, Maria and I. We're best friends."

"That sounds like the best relationship to me."

"Maybe it is the best place to start." He studied her, his tremors noticeable in the stillness. "How are you doing?"

"I'm…" She nodded, unable to speak. After a moment she cleared her throat. "Good. I'm good. I'm happy here. I'm getting settled, and I think good things are happening."

"Your relationship with Joe?"

"He's a good man. Better than I deserve. We're not getting married, Dad. You know that, right?"

He smiled at the admission. "A father can hope."

"I'm never getting married."

"I'm sorry to hear that," Joe said from somewhere in the shadowy area of the yard.

"Eavesdropper," she accused.

"Didn't mean to," Joe said as he joined them on the patio. "I came to check on you."

"I'm still standing."

"Yes, you are."

Jack grabbed his walker and pushed himself to his feet. "I think I'll go on in. It's starting to get cool, even with the fire. There are fajitas in the fridge if you're hungry. Maria said to tell you there's cheesecake, too. She made it this morning."

Daisy stood to wish her father good-night, kissing him on the cheek. He patted her back and called her his "Never Back Down Daisy," before going inside.

Joe took the seat her father had abandoned.

She didn't want to talk to him. She didn't want to discuss what he'd overheard.

"Could we just not do this tonight?" she asked.

"Sure, that's fair."

His tone said, not tonight, but soon. And when it all ended, what then? When Joe was not her fake fiancé and the twins went home to Lindsey, what would her life look like then?

They sat outside until the night air grew cold

and coyotes howled in the distance. They didn't speak. At some point Joe reached for her hand and she let him hold it, thankful for the warmth and the friendship without strings.

If that was all they ever had, she'd be grateful.

But a part of her, deep down, definitely wanted more than that.

Chapter Ten

Sunday afternoon Daisy followed Jack and Maria into the fellowship hall of Hope Community Church. She immediately searched the room for Joe and spotted him with his grandmother. They were placing pies on a long table where other pies had been left for the auction. He spotted her and waved. She acknowledged him with a nod and wave, then moved on, pushing the twins in their stroller because it was easier than trying to carry two almost one-year-old girls.

"That was a pretty cold greeting," Kylie said as she slipped up next to her. "I mean, he's your fiancé, isn't he?"

Daisy started to deny it but then didn't. "I'll see him in a bit. Is there something I should be doing?"

"Not right now. We'll have the pie auction in about an hour, and then we'll serve dinner."

"I'll take the twins to the nursery. Maybe I can help out there?"

"That would be fantastic. I'll come check on you or have someone come get you so you can take part in the pie auction."

Daisy tugged at the scarf she'd wrapped around her neck. It sometimes felt so tight and suffocating. Sometimes it itched.

Kylie dragged her gaze away from the scarf and held her gaze. "You don't have to hide who you are or what you've been through."

"I know. I should go. To the nursery."

"Daisy," Kylie called out as her sister-in-law maneuvered the stroller toward the nursery.

"Don't worry. I'm fine. And later we can talk. About everything. Just not right now."

Pushing the stroller down the narrow hall, she found the nursery. The other worker was rocking a baby as she smiled up at Daisy.

"Well, hello there, Daisy West. Look at you and your two beautiful little girls. Are you leaving them with me?"

"I thought I'd help out here, if that's all right?"

"I'd love the help. It'll get busy in a bit, and one of our nursery workers called in sick. You can take the girls out of their stroller and put it in the storage closet. The one on the left. The right is the Christmas closet."

"Thank you." She pulled Myra out first and

sat her on the floor in front of a toy piano. As she pulled Miriam out, she turned to the worker. "Do I know you?"

"Land's sake, I would think so. I'm Mrs. Tanner. You were in my first grade class."

First grade... Mrs. Tanner? Daisy finally remembered. Mrs. Ilene Tanner had read them stories and brought them snacks to take home on weekends.

"I remember you." She smiled as she said it. "I knew, even then, that you loved the Lord."

"Well, that is the sweetest compliment you could ever give me."

From down the hall they heard raised voices.

"What in the world?" Daisy placed Miriam on the floor with Myra and sidled up toward the door, instantly on alert.

She hated the way her stomach ached when she heard arguing. She despised the way it triggered her, made her want to curl up in a ball and hide. Over time she'd learned to face her fears, but it still affected her.

"I'm *not* going to be Santa Claus. No way," one angry male voice announced.

"Tell every kid within ear shot, why don't you?" The other voice held a hint of laughter. "Come on, you're perfect. I mean, if Santa was the Grinch, you'd be perfect. And you had a couple of weeks to pack on a few extra pounds."

"I'm not the Grinch, either." She knew that voice. She knew them both.

When they rounded the corner, she ducked back into the nursery, covering her mouth to keep from laughing out loud.

"It isn't funny," Joe called down the hall. "I'm not exactly the size, age or temperament for this job."

She leaned back out the door. "You're perfect."

She shouldn't have called out to him because he came to a stop in the hall to look at her. And next to him, Isaac seemed just as interested.

"Thank you for noticing." He winked as he said it.

"You are most definitely *not* perfect," she told him. "I mean for the job, yes. You could definitely be him. That, um…*person* you were speaking about earlier."

She smiled at a mother and daughter who were heading for the nursery. The mother looked worried. The daughter looked curious.

"Will you be my Mrs.?" he asked, knowing he was trying not to give it away to listening children.

"Me, your Mrs.? I don't think so."

Isaac laughed. "I think we all know that you're already applying for the role, so you might as well do this. Consider it on the job training."

"I'm not—" She bit back her reply because she'd almost announced she wasn't marrying him. "I'm not going to do this."

"I will if you will," Joe teased.

"I'm not going to discuss this with you. And by then…"

They both knew. The sham of an engagement would be over. It needed to end soon. Her conscience was bothering her. She liked Joe's family and didn't want to hurt them. She didn't want to be hurt.

Joe slowly backed away. "If you agree to be Mrs. Claus, I'll agree to be Santa. It will make it way more fun."

"Go away. I have to help with the nursery."

They were still flirting with each other when Holly's waitress, Leena, came down the hall. She ducked her head as she approached them and tried to sneak past Daisy into the nursery. She had a little girl with her. A pretty toddler with blond hair and delicate features that were far too sad for a little girl her age. She might have been two years old.

"Leena, how are you doing?" Joe asked as the waitress squeezed through the door, keeping her back to them.

"I'm good, Joe. Thank you for asking."

Joe shook his head and pointed to his eye. Daisy nodded. "Is there a sign up sheet, Mrs. Tanner?" she asked.

Mrs. Tanner nodded toward the table by the door. "Yes, there is. She needs to put her little one's age, Mom's name and phone number and who can check the child out of the nursery."

Daisy grabbed the clipboard before Leena could get to it. She held it out to her, and Leena took it without ever raising her head.

"Leena, are you okay?" Daisy asked the waitress. "I can help you."

"I'm fine." Leena attempted a smile, but the movement seemed to cause her pain. "I fell walking up my own steps. I think because I'm pregnant I'm extra clumsy."

Her hand went to her belly.

"Congratulations on the baby." Daisy continued to hold the clipboard that the other woman had already filled out. She understood women like Leena. She had been Leena, once. She'd made excuses for her bruises. She'd learned to take the blame, to accept that it had been because of her behavior. Her husband had manipulated her into believing that he cared for her, protected her and provided for her. And that she angered him to the point of abuse. According to him, it had always been her fault.

Daisy closed her eyes briefly, praying for

strength. She tugged at the scarf around her neck, loosening it, letting it drift to the floor. Leena's eyes came up, curious. Daisy knew the moment she saw the scar and recognized it for what it was. They all had war injuries. She would guess Leena had scars she kept hidden. Sometimes scars were on the inside.

She leaned closer to the other woman. "Leena, I've been in your shoes. I can help."

Leena shook her head. "I have to go. I'm helping serve dinner. Please watch my baby."

"We'll watch your baby," Daisy promised as the other woman rushed down the hall. Her heart broke for Leena, for all of the Leenas of the world.

She wanted to rescue them all the way Becky had rescued her. If it hadn't been for Dixie's adoptive mother, she would never have survived.

"I've noticed her bruises," Mrs. Tanner said after a few minutes. "She was one of my kids, and it breaks my heart. I've tried talking to her, to offer help. She's strong and won't listen."

Daisy shook her head. "She isn't strong, she's falling apart on the inside and trying her best to survive. I'm sorry, that sounded rude."

"No, it sounded as if it came from someone who understands Leena far better than I or anyone else who has tried to help. Maybe you're the one who can finally help her, Daisy."

"In the end it's up to her." Daisy sank to the floor next to the twins, thinking not only of Leena but of their mother, and the choices she was making for herself and her daughters each and every day.

A knock on the door drew her attention, and she smiled as Joe stepped into the room. "Problem solved. I'm Santa. You're my helper. Isaac always gets his way."

She didn't know what to say. Joe sank to the floor next to her.

"You okay?" he asked.

"I'm good. Just thinking about Leena."

"I thought so." He brushed the hair back behind her ear. "She has to want help."

"She has to know that help is here for her."

"That's true." He sat next to her, his presence comforting and frightening all at the same time. Frightening because she had grown used to him. They had played at being a couple for a little over a week, and somehow it had started to seem real, as if they really were engaged.

"We have to end this, you know," she whispered.

"I know," he whispered back, touching his forehead to hers. Their words were just between the two of them.

But the heartache she felt was hers alone.

* * *

Joe knew that for the rest of the evening, Daisy would try to avoid him. He didn't plan on allowing that to happen. When she surfaced for the pie auction, he waved her over. The Lawsons were sharing a large table with the Wests. She would have to join them or sit with strangers.

She gave him a perturbed look and then glanced around the room.

Clearly, she was seriously considering sitting with strangers. She headed in the opposite direction, stopped, then came over to him. Her grin proved she'd been messing with him.

"I saved you a seat," he told her, pulling the chair out.

"I know you did. But I wanted to make it clear, I choose my own seat, Mr. Lawson."

"You're a stubborn woman, Mrs. Claus."

"Very funny." She sat down, and he took the seat next to hers. His grandmother sat on her right side. That seemed to make both women happy. They had bonded, his grandmother and Daisy. Interesting.

"Did you see the pie my grandson baked?" Nana El asked.

"I did," Daisy responded. "It looks suspiciously like one of Holly's pecan pies."

"Does it? Maybe they use the same recipe. I have it on very good authority that it's a very good pecan pie."

"If it is anything like Holly's, I can vouch for that. Holly makes the most amazing pecan pie. Sometimes she puts chocolate chips in her pies."

"Could we please stop discussing Holly's chocolate chip pie," Joe said, leaning in close to his fake fiancée.

It was a mistake, getting that close. It meant catching a whiff of her fruity shampoo. It meant his cheek barely, just barely, brushing the soft strands of her dark hair. He needed a reality check.

"Where are the twins?"

"In the nursery. They'll be there until this event is over. The other workers arrived, and they told me to come join the fun. They'll have meals brought to the nursery. If they need me, they'll call."

Then, suddenly, the bidding started.

"Are all of these pies made by men?" she asked, clearly perplexed.

"The men in the church practice their pie-baking skills all year long," Joe informed her. "You'll notice it doesn't hurt the bidding at all. This auction brings in a large portion of the money used for the Community Christmas. Most of tonight's donations for meals and pies will go toward next year's expenses. And it's a good time for us to all come together, socialize and do good for people who are our neighbors."

"Why do they do the pie auction before the dinner?"

"So you can eat dinner with the pie baker of your choice, if you like."

"They put a lot of thought into this."

"They have to. This brings in enough money to buy gifts, coats, shoes and other items for about two hundred area children."

The auctioneer picked up a pie and grinned. Joe knew what was coming. "This pecan pie says it was made by Joe Lawson. Now, I'm not saying Joe would lie, but this looks a lot like the same pecan pie Holly serves at the café. At least we know it'll be good." Everyone in the room laughed.

Then the bidding started. Next to him, Daisy sat with her hands still in her lap. Whoever bid for the pie, Cassidy upped the price by bidding double the going rate. Sitting across from them, she smiled as if she'd already won.

Daisy gave him a wink, then raised her hand to join the bidding. The crowd went wild. The price of the pie climbed and climbed. Daisy considered backing out but she was committed to winning. Cassidy seemed just as determined.

"I'm not sure if they realize they're bidding on the pie, not Joe," Isaac spoke up. Loudly. Too loudly.

Daisy started to lower her hand but then she

raised it again. Joe caught Cassidy's gaze and she gave a slow nod and a wink. Daisy called out an amount that was the highest bid of the night and the pie was hers.

"Show off," Joe whispered.

"I don't like to lose," she told him.

The pie was delivered to their table. Nana El patted Daisy's hand. "That's the way to do it, girl."

A streak of red creeped up Daisy's neck.

"Are you going to share that pie?" Joe asked, while batting his eyelashes and flashing his most charming grin.

"I don't like to lose. I also don't like to share," she teased back.

"I'm taking this pie and my fiancée, and we're going to have a private picnic," he announced to everyone.

She glanced up at him as he stood and took the pie from her. "What are you doing? I don't think this is how it works."

"Come with me," he told her.

All around them people were staring, mouths wide open, questions in their eyes. Isaac West started to stand, but Rebecca pulled him back to his seat.

He'd taken a chance that Daisy would deny him, or finally confess about their phony engagement. She was too brave and too bold for that. She stood, grabbed her purse and said something to Nana El about her misbehaving grandson.

Nana El actually looked worried. He leaned around Daisy and winked at his grandmother.

He carried the pie in his left hand and put his right arm across her back to guide her from the building.

"Where are we going?" she asked as they stepped into the cool December night. The sky was dark and the stars were like millions of jewels sprinkled across midnight blue velvet.

"I'm not sure. I didn't think that far ahead when I—"

"Made a spectacle of yourself?" she interrupted, finishing for him.

"Yes, maybe that's what I did. But I didn't want to sit in there and play a part anymore."

"And what part were you playing?" she asked as they stood in the center of the churchyard.

All around them Christmas lights twinkled from trees up and down the street. The town of Hope was decorated for the holidays. It was romantic and beautiful, if he did say so himself. Especially with Christmas carols drifting from the speakers located in the shopping area a few blocks away.

"We're playing the part of a loving and engaged couple, aren't we?" He realized he didn't really like it. He wasn't good at playacting.

"Is that what we're doing?"

"Yes." He spoke softly because she'd lowered her voice. "I think that's what we're doing. And honestly, I don't care about this pie."

He set it on a nearby bench.

"I wanted to eat that pie," she told him. "I paid a lot of money for it."

"I'll buy you two pies tomorrow."

"Will they be $500 pies?"

He placed his left hand on her cheek. He waited to see if she would pull away, because he'd respect that. Respect her. He didn't want to push.

But she didn't pull away.

"I want to kiss you," he whispered in her ear.

She smiled up at him. "I wouldn't have guessed."

He laughed a little. "But I want it to be okay with you."

"I think you should. We can't waste the lights and music or the star-filled sky, so I think you should kiss me." Her hand came to rest on his cheek. "Please kiss me, Joe."

This was different from a quick kiss good-night or a stolen moment. This kiss mattered. He wanted it to matter to them both.

Slowly he touched his lips to hers. He thought he might be close to falling in love with her. He was a grown man and he knew better, but in the moment, maybe he didn't have a clue.

Her kiss unraveled his good sense and made him think that holding her was definitely the closest he'd ever come to being in love. In that kiss he forgot that everything between them was make-believe.

As he moved to gather her closer, she pulled away, her lips still parted, her eyes damp with tears. He wanted to see so much in her eyes. The last thing he expected to see were her tears.

"Regrets?" he asked.

"We can't do that again." Her words were thick with emotion.

Choosing to keep it simple and let her explain, he said, "I guess I'm confused. I thought you wanted that."

"I did. Oh Joe, I don't know," she told him. Again, her eyes filled with tears. "I don't want to hurt you, and I don't want to lead you on."

She picked up the pie he'd left on the bench and walked away, disappearing into a side door of the church. Probably going to collect the twins. She would no doubt leave the dinner. And him.

Something amazing had happened between them, and her fear was chasing her away.

The question was, would he chase after her? Or let her leave forever?

Chapter Eleven

Two days later, Mr. Peterson, the electrician, continued to explain as if he thought Daisy understood wiring and electricity. She nodded and made understanding noises, and he continued to talk. Unfortunately, somewhere in his explanation about types of wiring, proper connections and grounding, her mind wandered to Sunday evening and the kiss.

She couldn't stop reliving the moment when Joe asked permission to kiss her. And she'd said yes. Whatever had come over her to say yes?

"You understand this job could take two weeks?" the electrician asked. He wore that look on his face, the one that said he thought a woman wouldn't understand anything he said.

She gathered her wits and put on her best businesswoman face. "Yes, of course, I understand."

"No electricity in this house for two weeks. If we have a cold snap, your pipes might freeze up."

"That's reassuring," she muttered.

He gave her a hard look over the top of his wire-framed glasses. "This is serious, ma'am."

"I know that it is. I really am listening. I'm disappointed, but I understand that it will take time to do this right."

"It's a good house. We'll get this taken care of for you."

"And when did you say you could start?"

"I think I should…" A knock on the back door interrupted him. He quirked a brow at her and again looked over the top of his glasses.

"When?"

"I have to finish the job I'm on. I'm hoping by Thursday I can get that finished up."

"So really…"

The knock on the door grew more insistent.

"I should get this."

"I think that would be wise. I'll gather up my tools, and I'll leave a bill on the kitchen counter."

"Thank you, Mr. Peterson."

She hurried to the back door. A woman stood on the porch, her back to Daisy, but the hair, blond with lavender highlights, looked familiar. As Daisy opened the door, the woman turned and Daisy gasped at the woman's bruised and swollen face.

Leena Parker, Holly's waitress, tried to smile but began to cry. Great heaving sobs shook her body. Her daughter held tight to her hand, blond ringlets framing her pale, frightened face. The first thing Daisy needed to do was to calm Leena so that her daughter wouldn't be afraid.

"Leena, come inside."

Leena hesitated. "I don't know. Maybe this was a bad idea."

"No, it wasn't. Please come in."

Leena trembled as she glanced toward the road. "He'll be…"

Daisy picked up the shivering little girl. "Let's go in the house."

Leena followed her inside. Daisy led her to the sitting room off her bedroom. She trusted her electrician with her home wiring, not with stories of women coming to her back door. She was sure he was a very nice man, but the last thing they needed was for Leena's husband to find out she was here.

"Sit for a minute and just breathe." Daisy pointed to a settee, and as Leena sat, Daisy handed her a blanket. "I'm going to get you something for the pain and an ice pack. Does your little girl need a snack?"

Leena nodded and drew her daughter close, covering them both with the blanket.

"I'm sorry it's so cold. My electricity is out of commission." Where would she put them if she couldn't keep them here?

"Thank you. We left without eating lunch, and we walked all the way over."

"Oh, Leena, you should have called me. Let me get you both something to eat."

"I couldn't," Leena told her. "My jaw. I don't think it's…" She looked at her daughter and didn't finish the sentence, but they both knew what she'd meant to say. She didn't think her jaw was broken.

What kind of monster did this to his wife? Unfortunately, she knew the answer to that question. She'd been married to one.

"I'll be right back," she promised as she left them to comfort each other.

Her electrician had left, and she found the promised invoice under her salt and pepper shakers. She glanced over the itemized list, but she didn't want to dwell on it. The idea of being out of her home for more than two weeks wasn't something she wanted to dwell on at the moment.

She didn't have much in the house but she found a bag of cheese puffs, a bottle of water and, after rummaging in her purse, a bottle of ibuprofen. She placed everything on a tray, but before she returned to her sitting room, she double checked the locks on the doors. She didn't want to take a chance that anyone could sneak up on them.

When she entered the sitting room, Leena and Daphne were curled up together. Daphne sucked her thumb and twirled her hair while Leena rubbed her bare feet. The little girl with her pixie face and blond curls blinked sleepily but smiled around the thumb in her mouth.

"I brought a snack, water, and medicine." She set the tray on the coffee table.

Leena opened the cheese puffs and handed them to her little girl. Daphne sat up, her little hand reaching into the bag as she smiled up at Daisy.

"Take these." Daisy handed the ibuprofen and water to Leena.

"Thank you," Leena said after swallowing the pills.

"How did you know to come here?"

"You said you would help me. And I'm tired of pretending this is okay. I need help. I don't want my little girl growing up thinking this is normal. I don't want to lose my baby." At the words, her hand went to her belly and more tears streamed down her bruised cheeks.

"This is an important step, Leena. It won't be easy."

"I know it won't. I've tried to leave him more than once, and I've always gone back. He apologizes and promises not to do it again. Or he convinces me it was my fault. But I know it isn't my fault and he's going to do it again. Promises don't change him."

"I'll do whatever I can to help. But we can't do this here, without electricity or heat." She sat down on the chair opposite them. "I'm not sure what to do."

"I could go somewhere else."

"Do you have somewhere else to go?"

Leena shook her head. "No, I don't. My parents live in Indiana. They don't have the money or a way to help. His family lives in Oklahoma City. We came here so he could find work."

"Then we'll figure this out. I think we'll start by going to Mercy Ranch. Is that okay with you?"

"Do you think Mr. West will mind?" Leena moved closer to her daughter.

"He won't mind. As a matter of fact, he'll be more understanding than you could imagine." She stood, smiling down at mother and daughter. "That's actually the perfect plan. I'll pull my car up to the back door, and we'll get ready to go. I need to head back out there anyway. I'm not used to being away from the twins. They might not miss me, but I miss them."

Her phone rang as she walked out the back door. When she glanced at the caller ID, her first instinct was to ignore the call. But she couldn't. The twins' caseworker called midweek for a reason. She felt a heavy sense of dread as she answered.

"Daisy, it's Cheryl Morgan. I'm sorry to bother you, and I know this call is unexpected. I have some news."

"Good news or bad?" Daisy asked.

"It depends on your perspective."

It was going to be bad. Daisy could tell by Cheryl's tone. She continued toward her car, holding the phone to her ear.

"Lindsey's lawyer asked the judge to look at her case and reconsider visits. The judge looked at everything and decided she's been doing fairly well until this past month or so. It's the holidays and he's feeling generous. And she has the apartment and a part-time job."

Daisy closed her eyes as the world collapsed around her. This was what they'd been working for, she reminded herself. She wanted Lindsey better. She wanted the twins back with their mother. It was meant to be this way. Wasn't it?

She drew in a sharp and achy breath. "Okay, so what does that mean?"

"The twins will spend a night with their mother."

"Unsupervised?"

"Unsupervised," the caseworker confirmed. "One day next week. I'm not sure which one. I'll call when I know. If you can bring them to my office, that would be great. We'll drive them over to Lindsey's apartment."

"Okay, I can do that."

"They're going to be fine, Daisy."

She nodded, but her throat had tightened and she couldn't speak.

"Daisy, you okay?"

She took a deep breath. "Yes, I'm good. And I know they'll be okay."

Without thinking, she'd walked to the field where her horse had grazed. He was gone now. They'd taken him to Mercy Ranch so he wouldn't be on this property alone. The chickens were a different story. They clucked and squawked from their pen. From the racket, she guessed one was probably laying an egg. She'd been out to feed and water them each day but so far there hadn't been eggs.

The twins were going to their mother for a night. She told herself to be happy for them, and for Lindsey. Instead, she thought about the little things. The twins didn't really know Lindsey and she didn't know them. What if they woke up in the middle of the night? What if she didn't feed them what they liked and they were hungry?

The thoughts did her no good. She remembered a Bible verse she'd recently heard. Worry wouldn't add a cubit to her stature. It wouldn't change anything for her or the twins.

Right now she had to deal with the problem at hand. She had to help Leena. She got in the rental SUV and pulled close to the back of the house. She would get Leena to Mercy Ranch, then she would think about the twins and this visit with their mother.

Leena had been watching for her. As Daisy pulled to a stop, the young mother hurried from the house, her little girl in her arms. They climbed in the back seat together and buckled their seat belts.

"How far did you walk?" Daisy asked as they pulled out on the road.

"It's about two miles. That's why we only have the one bag. I knew I had to leave while my husband was at work."

"We'll make sure the two of you have what you need," Daisy assured the other woman.

It took less than ten minutes to drive to Mercy Ranch. When they arrived, Daphne was asleep, curled up against her mother in the back seat of the SUV.

As she stepped out of the vehicle, she caught

herself glancing toward the stable. Joe's truck was parked next to Isaac's. She caught herself longing for him to walk out of the barn. She found herself needing him. She needed to tell him about the electrical situation, about the call from the caseworker, and about Leena.

She needed to end this relationship. What had started on a whim was beginning to feel too real. She didn't want to need someone in her life.

As she helped Leena and her daughter from the car, the bruises on Leena's face were a reminder of why she would never again marry. Once upon a time, a young woman named Leena had fallen in love and gotten married. She'd probably trusted that the man she'd joined her life to would always be her prince.

Unfortunately, fairy tales sometimes turned out to be nightmares. With that reminder she led Leena toward her father's house, hoping the young mom would be strong enough to make a break from the man who had abused her.

Daisy paused at the door and glanced back at the barn to see Joe backing his truck up to a trailer. As he got out of the truck he waved and she walked through the door.

Joe had planned to leave for his new property but when he'd seen Daisy pull up with Leena in the car, he'd decided to wait. Something told him Daisy would need him. He caught two horses and put them in the corral. Next, he loaded tack in his horse trailer.

He watched as Daisy led Leena and Daphne to the "women's apartment" a short distance from Jack's house. The apartment was a remodeled garage. Kylie West had once lived there. So had Sierra and Eve. They were all married and gone now. Well, Kylie still lived in Hope, so did Sierra. Eve lived on a ranch a short distance away.

With time to kill, he decided to work with a gelding Jack had bought a few weeks back. The horse had come to them with some bad habits. That was the type of horse Jack seemed to like buying, the ones that needed rehabilitating. But then, the whole ranch had been built to make broken lives new again.

The horse, a dark chestnut with wicked teeth, turned to nip at Joe as he led him from the stall. Joe held tight to the lead rope and led the horse to the arena. He kept the horse close and the lead rope short.

When they reached the center of the arena, Joe gave the horse some length on the lunge line and whistled. The horse started in a wide circle around Joe. He let the animal continue for several minutes, then cued him to stop. The horse stomped his feet but remained standing. Joe walked up to him.

"There you go, big guy. Not so bad." He ran his arm over the horse's back, standing close to him.

He was making progress, it just took time. Some animals had been abused and neglected. It took a while to build their trust.

Jack didn't tolerate "bucking a horse out." That meant they weren't putting on a rodeo, tossing a saddle on a frightened animal and making him buck until he couldn't buck anymore.

Jack treated people the same way he treated hurt and abused animals. He gave them time. He let them feel safe.

It had taken Joe time to get used to his new life, his change of circumstances. A few years ago, he wouldn't have attempted working a horse like this one. Holding the lead with his left arm while calming the animal. A few years ago, he hadn't trusted himself too much.

"Nice horse," a voice called from outside the arena.

Definitely not Daisy's voice. He turned the animal and faced his visitor.

"Dad, I didn't expect you out here today. I thought you all were going shopping in Tulsa?"

"The women went." His dad opened the gate

and stepped into the arena. "They took Cassidy to the airport on the way."

"I'm sorry I didn't get a chance to tell her good-bye," he said.

His dad laughed. "Let's both be honest, son. I messed up, bringing her here. I don't know, I guess I thought if you saw an old friend, it'd make you homesick and perhaps you would want to come home."

"Dad, this is my home now. I'm going to stay here, build a house and a life."

"With Daisy?"

"I'm not sure about that."

His dad nodded, as if he knew.

"Dad, we're not really engaged."

"I kind of guessed she was saving you from our bad attempt at matchmaking."

They both laughed and the tension eased. The air cleared somewhat. It hadn't always been this tense between them. Growing up, Joe had been close to his dad. They'd gone to ball games together, fished, fixed things. The tension had started when he joined the Army after college graduation, then had decided to stay at Mercy Ranch rather than return home to Connecticut.

"Dad, I left because I wanted to be my own person, not the newest member of Lawson and Associates."

His dad brushed a hand down the horse's

neck, causing the skittish animal to snort and nip at his arm.

"I wouldn't do that if I were you," Joe warned.

His dad took a step back. "I wanted you to follow the easier path."

"The easier path for you. But it wasn't my path," Joe explained as he leaned against the horse, wrapping his right arm over the animal's back. He felt the horse tense but he remained there, talking and soothing him until he calmed down.

"But now you're returning to that path, as a lawyer."

"On my own terms. Dad, I couldn't have come home to Connecticut. I was a lot like this horse. I was afraid all the time, having nightmares, unsure of myself and everyone around me. I had to figure out how to live my life again, and the last thing I wanted, even if it was well-meaning, was for my family to tell me the best way to go about my future."

"You could have told us all that, you know."

Joe chuckled. "I think I tried."

"You probably did."

"Mercy Ranch gave me back my confidence. Coming here, I learned skills I never knew I had, and I learned patience with myself and other people. And with animals, too."

His dad nodded, slowly, accepting. It was

something Joe had been waiting for. It had taken years, but finally there was acceptance and forgiveness.

"Your mom would like to have you and Daisy, as well as those twin babies, over to the house for dinner."

"I think it's time we tell everyone the truth." The announcement came from outside the arena.

Joe sighed, knowing she was right. "Good to see you, too, Daisy."

"I think we already know the truth," Joe's dad told her. "That doesn't mean we don't want to have you over for dinner."

Joe led the horse to the gate but kept a careful eye on Daisy. She looked as if this day had been tough. She looked emotionally beat up.

Fortunately, Joe's dad noticed something was off. He gave Daisy a careful look before turning back to Joe. "I'm going to go on now. Your mother and grandmother will be back from shopping soon, and we're supposed to try the restaurant at the resort."

"You'll enjoy it." Joe led the horse through the open gate. "At some point this week I'd like to show you the office I've bought, and my land."

"Maybe later this afternoon?" his father suggested.

Joe had other plans for today. Plans that included making sure Daisy was okay. "No, not today. Maybe tomorrow?"

"Of course." Joe's dad gave Daisy a hug. "Where are those two girls of yours?"

"With Maria. She's feeding them junk food as we speak."

Joe walked with his dad out of the stable, then returned to put the horse back in a stall. Daisy waited for him, her expression more pensive than usual. He guessed this went deeper than Leena's situation.

"Are you okay?" he asked.

"I'm not great," she admitted. "I just left Leena and her little girl Daphne in the women's apartment. Kylie is going to meet with Leena and talk to her. Later, after they rest."

"Do you want to go for a ride?" he asked as he watered the gelding and made sure he had enough hay.

"Horseback?" she asked.

"Of course. I have two horses ready to load. Their tack is already on the trailer. I thought I'd show you the land I bought."

"You bought land?"

"I did. I know Jack would let me stay on at Mercy Ranch forever, but it's time for me to find a place of my own."

Together they loaded horses, her gray Arab and his quarter horse, on the trailer he'd already hooked up to his truck. While Daisy went to the house to check on Maria and the girls, Joe tossed some bottled water in a cooler and grabbed a couple of protein bars. When she returned, he was ready to go.

"All set?" he asked as he went to open the passenger side door for her.

"I'm ready," she said, climbing inside the truck, then pulling the door closed.

"Tell me about your land and the house you want to build. Tell me what kind of law you want to practice," she told him as they pulled down the drive.

"Family law," he told her. "And the land is several hundred acres, pasture with some woods."

"It sounds perfect."

Silence fell over them until they reached the farm. He drove down the long driveway, fenced on both sides, to the spot where there'd once been a farmhouse. There were a few big trees, the remains of a barn and a good well.

"This is where I plan to build a house."

Daisy finally spoke. "I remember this place. The house was still standing when I was a kid. I think we visited here."

"Maybe," Joe told her. "Jack knew the family that had lived here. I think they might have been distant cousins of yours."

"Possibly."

They got out of the truck, and she led the gray gelding from the trailer, saddling him without speaking. He wasn't surprised. Joe led his horse out and followed suit.

She mounted the gray, then, without looking back, she took off across the field, her dark hair flying behind her. Jack pushed his hat down firmly on his head, mounted up and raced after her. She didn't slow until she came to a stand of trees at the western edge of the property. She eased her horse to a trot and Joe rode up next to her.

"Feel better?" he asked.

"No," she told him. She pulled the scarf at her neck, releasing the colorful cloth and yanking it loose. She shoved it under her leg.

He settled in next to her as they rode along the fence line.

"They want me to take the twins to Lindsey's apartment for an overnight visit. It will happen one day next week, and I guess I'm not ready for it. I went into this thinking I would help a friend. I thought it would be easy. I thought it wouldn't hurt."

"You love them. It makes sense that it would hurt."

"What if she hurts them? I keep thinking of all the ways she could mess this up and how that would affect those two little girls that I've grown to love. In my heart, they're mine. But they're not. Not really. And I know I'm not supposed to feel this way."

"I would worry about you if you *didn't* feel this way, Daisy."

"Of course," she whispered, pulling the scarf from under her leg and wiping her eyes. "This really stinks."

She dismounted and he joined her, walking beside her. Afraid of saying the wrong thing, he remained silent for the moment.

They walked, each leading their horse, until they reached the pond. The air was cool but the sun felt warm. Daisy closed her eyes and took a deep breath. Joe watched her, wishing he could do something to take away the sadness he saw in her expression. He'd never felt this way about anyone before. And he was both thrilled and a lot scared.

Also, it was unexpected, this overpowering need to fix everything for her.

"I'll do whatever I can to help," Joe told her.

"Call a plumber or an electrician," she teased, reminding of what he'd offered before.

"I can definitely do those things. But if you need more, I can do that, too. If you'd like, I'll go with you when you take the twins to

Lindsey's place. And I'll do what I can to help Leena."

She nodded. "I don't know if anyone has ever told you how nice your voice is. Make all the promises you want, but it's your voice that makes me feel safe."

Heat climbed into his cheeks. He seriously hadn't blushed in more than a dozen years. Not this kind of blush.

"Sorry, cowboy, didn't mean to embarrass you."

"And yet you did." He took off his hat and hooked it on the horn of his horse's saddle.

"And yet I did," she echoed as she studied his face.

Without the scarf, she had a beautiful neck. Her scar didn't take away from who she was or her beauty.

"You shouldn't wear the scarf," he told her.

"So I've been told before. But when people see the scar, that's all they see."

"I don't. I see you." He leaned closer to her, dropping the reins of his horse and knowing the animal would stay put. "I see the remarkable, strong woman who isn't afraid to help others. She isn't afraid to conquer her fears. She deals with life head-on." He took hold of her.

"She's a coward," she whispered as she stepped into his arms.

"She's remarkable." He continued to hold her,

and she didn't pull away. "She's afraid to trust, but she loves the people in her life and cares about them. I think that's why she holds back. Because she loves them and doesn't want to be hurt by them."

She closed her eyes. "Stop, Joe."

He kissed her, and she wrapped her arms around his neck and kissed him back. In that moment he made the decision to win her heart, and prove to her that he was a man who could be trusted to love her.

Forever.

Chapter Twelve

Daisy moved back into her home a little over a week after the electrician had given her the dismal news about her home's electrical problems. Leena and Daphne moved in with her. And it was on that Tuesday she got the call that the twins' visit with their mother was scheduled for the next day. A part of her wanted to run away.

But the grown-up, responsible Daisy did as the state ordered. It was the hardest thing she'd ever done. On Wednesday morning she loaded the twins, a bag of clothes, diapers and bottles, plus a few toys, in the SUV for the drive to Tulsa. She didn't tell Joe. She didn't want to lean on him for support. She didn't want to lean on anyone. From the beginning she'd known this day would happen. Now it was time to face this. Alone.

She drove to Tulsa, to the caseworker's office.

She put the twins in the caseworker's car, and together they went to Lindsey's new apartment. Daisy couldn't make herself keep up small talk with Cheryl, the caseworker. It wasn't the other woman's fault. This had always been the plan, to reunite the twins with their mother. Even if only for short periods of time. The short visits would lead to permanency.

All of that knowledge didn't undo the pain.

She remained quiet, trying not to cry. She didn't cry as she carried Miriam up the steps to the tiny apartment that Lindsey had been able to rent with the income from her part-time job. She didn't cry when she saw the bed with the stained quilt and torn stuffed animals.

It wasn't about the things Lindsey could or couldn't give her daughters. Daisy only wanted to know that they would be safe.

"I can do this," Lindsey said.

Daisy nodded. "I know you can, Lindsey, I know you. I used to trust you with my business."

"But you don't trust me with my own daughters."

She took a deep breath before answering. "I just want what's best for the three of you," she said.

Lindsey looked tired. Defeated, even as she smiled and tried to look as if she could be the mom that Myra and Miriam needed.

Lindsey held Myra, because she'd always been the easier twin. The little girl played with her mother's hair and chewed on her own thumb as she jabbered and grinned.

"She got a tooth," Lindsey noted. "I missed that."

Daisy's heart ached. "Yes, they have teeth."

The words hung between them. Daisy suddenly wished she hadn't been so stubborn and had asked Kylie or Rebecca or even Jack to come with her.

Or Joe. She blinked back tears, refusing to allow herself to want him to be the one standing next to her. But she realized she wanted him with her more than anyone else.

That made him the biggest danger of them all.

"You have bottles, formula, food and diapers?" Cheryl asked Lindsey. "Can you show it all to me one last time?"

"Of course," Lindsey answered. "Right in here."

She showed them everything the caseworker asked about. "I bought macaroni and cheese, just like Daisy said."

"Good job, Lindsey." Cheryl smiled. "We'll turn the girls over to you now, and we will be back tomorrow morning at ten."

"Tomorrow morning at ten. No problem." Lindsey reached for Miriam.

The little girl clung to Daisy's neck.

"Mama," Miriam sobbed, holding tight as the caseworker pulled her free from Daisy and handed her to Lindsey.

"Daisy, I'm sorry." Lindsey moved toward her as she held both girls, who were crying now.

"Just take care of them. Please," Daisy implored her.

"I will. I promise." Lindsey stood there with the twins as Daisy and Cheryl left.

Daisy didn't cry until she was alone in her car, driving back to Hope. Leaving the babies felt like leaving a piece of herself in that apartment. She wanted to believe they would be safe. She wanted to trust Lindsey to do the right thing.

It was barely noon when she pulled into her driveway. As she got out of the rental SUV, a truck pulled in behind her. Joe. She stood at the back of her vehicle, watching as he got out of his truck. He was tall, broad shouldered, a boulder of man with a smile that shifted from tender to heart-stopping at the drop of a hat. She'd never been more relieved to see anyone.

It would have been easier to feel annoyed or angry because he must have seen her drive through town and he'd followed her here. Checking up on her, obviously. He was pushy and overbearing and too protective. Exactly what she didn't want in her life.

"Are you okay?" he asked in that voice that rumbled and soothed all at the same time.

"I'm okay."

"You took the twins over to Lindsey's?"

She nodded, because if she said anything, the tears would start all over again, and she didn't want to cry. She didn't want him to think she needed him to rescue her. But she wanted to walk into his arms and let him hold her so badly right now. The thought made her angry with herself because it was the exact opposite of how she told herself she should feel.

He took matters into his own hands, closing the distance between them and wrapping his strong, left arm around her. "I would have gone with you," he said.

"I needed to do this alone."

"I know."

"It was the hardest thing I've ever done," she admitted. "I didn't know if I could do it. Miriam cried and wanted me. But I'm not her mama. I'm just the person who's taken care of her since she was an infant."

"You've been her mother," he assured her, still holding her close.

"But I'm not. And I don't know what to do with the empty space in my life, the one they filled up."

"Pray," he suggested. He kept his left arm

around her as they headed toward the house together.

"I'm not sure how. Does God really want to hear my prayers? I've yelled at Him and ignored Him for a big part of my life. Now that life is tough again, is it okay that I'm going to call out to Him to ask for help?"

"I think so," he said. "I can pray with you, if you'd like."

"Stop being so perfect. The man who rescues me, protects me and prays with me. What happens when I realize that you're just another person who'll disappoint me?" Or worse, hurt her.

"I'm human so I'm sure at some point I'll disappoint you. But I hope I never hurt you."

His words echoed her thoughts.

She reached for his hand. "You can pray for me."

He pulled off his hat and leaned forward, touching his forehead to hers. And he prayed out loud. He prayed for her, for Lindsey, for the twins. He prayed for peace and for faith.

She felt that peace wash over her, and as he prayed, she took a deep breath and allowed herself to believe.

"I need to do something," she told Joe when he'd finished and they approached the back door of the house. "I need to keep busy or else I'll worry about the girls too much."

"What do you want to do? I have a few hours before I have to meet my folks at the new office."

"I can't believe you're going to practice law in Hope."

"Every town needs a good lawyer."

"I know that's probably true. Thank you for helping Leena get that order of protection."

"It's a step in the right direction," he said. "But she still needs to pay attention to her surroundings and be vigilant."

Daisy nodded and opened the door, realizing what had just happened.

"You don't lock your doors?" Joe shook his head, and let out a long sigh. "Let's go over this again, about being safe and vigilant."

"You're right. I left the door unlocked, and I'm sure when Kylie left with Leena's daughter, Daphne, she did the same."

"I think if you want Faith House to be a home that helps abused women, you need to make a safety plan and have some safety steps."

"That's a good idea. Thank you."

He grinned.

"Would you like to help me decorate the Christmas trees?"

"You haven't decorated the trees yet? Are they still alive?"

"Of course, they are. I came over and watered

them a few times. The electrical problems really put a halt to all of my plans."

"Do you have decorations?" he asked as they entered the kitchen. "And coffee."

"The coffee maker is by the stove, and I've been assured by Mr. Peterson that we can use both appliances at the same time now. There's coffee in the basket next to the coffee maker."

"Do you want a cup?"

"I don't think so, I had a cup this morning before…" Suddenly the feelings came rushing back again. She felt lost and empty. Her breath caught, and she knew if she looked at him, she would cry.

"I'll make you a cup," he continued as if she hadn't rejected his offer. "And something to eat. I bet you didn't eat this morning."

She shook her head. "No, I didn't."

As she stood there trying to gather her thoughts, he came up behind her, his hand moving to hers, his strength a solid wall behind her. He kissed the top of her head.

"It's going to be okay. I know those are words and you need more than words right now, but it's all I have to give. It's truly what I believe."

She gave his hand a squeeze. "Thank you."

"How about an omelet. I'm very good at omelets. You'll be impressed, I promise."

He returned to the kitchen, and as she rummaged through the closet in the laundry room, she could hear him in her kitchen. He'd asked her virtual assistant to play a contemporary Christian song, and he started singing along. Once again, he'd arrived at just the right moment to rescue her.

Joe did make a decent omelet, if he said so himself. And since he usually cooked only for himself, he decided to try to adjust things to make enough for them both. He cracked the eggs with his left hand, a skill that had taken some time to develop, then mixed them. Next, he chopped up what he found in the fridge, a pepper, mushrooms, some precooked bacon and cheese, then poured it all together in the buttered pan.

Daisy returned with a large plastic container that she carried past him to the smaller of the two trees.

"I could have helped you," he called back to her.

"I can do this. Is that an omelet or scrambled eggs?"

He laughed as he looked at the pan. "It is indeed more scrambled than omelet. That doesn't mean it won't taste good. It all goes to the same place."

"I've heard that all my life, and I still don't

go for that theory. You can't convince me to eat a gross combination just because it all goes to the same place in the end."

He flipped the eggs. "I'll give you that."

"I'm starving," she admitted as he served her half the eggs in the pan. "I guess I hadn't realized how hungry I am."

"It's a good thing I showed up. You wouldn't have eaten and those poor trees wouldn't have gotten decorated."

"I want the lights on them. I want the twins to come home and see them all lit up."

"They will."

He sat next to her and they ate the eggs. Then he set the cup of coffee he'd made in front of her.

"This will make you feel better."

"Coffee always does," she told him. "Thank you for all of this. Most of all, thank you for being here. I thought I wanted to be alone, but I was wrong."

"Alone is lonely," he quipped. "It's good to have people we can count on to be there for us."

Trying to change the subject, she said, "My trees are so lonely without lights or ornaments. And you're tall, so you can put the star on top."

"I live to serve," he teased.

They did the dishes before starting to decorate the trees. She washed. He dried.

"I have my limits. Washing is not a job I've perfected. Believe me, no one wants imperfectly washed dishes. But I use a dishwasher."

"I have one but for a few dishes, it would take me a week to fill it up."

She had a question. He could see it in her eyes.

"What?"

She chewed on her bottom lip for a second. "I'm not sure how to ask."

"Just ask. I promise, I've answered a lot of questions."

"Okay. Why don't you have a prosthetic arm?"

"I do have one, and I use it sometimes. It's almost bionic. If I wore that thing all of the time, I really would be your superhero."

She blushed. "I never called you my superhero."

He winked, and grabbed the pan to put it in the dish drainer. "Maybe not, but you know I fit the role."

"Hmm, no, I don't think so. A hero maybe, not super."

"I'll take that."

She asked her next question. "Does it still bother you?"

"My arm? Not too much. There are things I can't do that I wish I could. But again, I do have the prosthetic. I do still have nightmares. Not as often as I used to."

"I'm sorry," she said, coming up on tiptoe to kiss his cheek. "You really are a superhero," she murmured.

"You're getting all mushy on me." He put the dish towel on the hook. "Let's decorate the trees."

He opened the tub she'd carried to the family room and together they went through the decorations.

"I think I want this tree to be red and gold," she mused. "And the one in the front sitting room will be blue and silver."

He gave her a look. "We're color coordinating the trees?"

"Of course. The furniture in this room is earth tones with some reds. The sitting room…"

He cut her off. "Blues and grays. Yes, I get it. I'm going to purposely hang different colored bulbs on your tree."

"I have a few that are different. I bought the twins each an ornament for their first Christmas."

Her phone rang as they were hanging lights. Daisy answered, giving him a look that told him it was something important.

"Hi, Lindsey, what is it?"

He could hear Lindsey's voice over the phone.

"They won't stop crying. It's only been a few hours, and they just won't stop and I can't make them. I tried. I tried to make them stop and I can't."

"Lindsey, you're the mom. You have to be calm. It's their first day with you. You have to give them time. Have you tried rocking them?"

"I tried rocking them. I tried a bottle and I tried food. I put them in that stupid stroller and I took them for a walk."

"Lindsey, I can't come get them."

Daisy scrunched her eyes and drew in a breath, and Joe knew what it cost her.

"Lindsey, you have to call Cheryl. I know this is hard, but this is part of being a mom. You can't quit just because they cry. They cried for me, too. Sometimes they don't sleep. It isn't always easy."

The voice on the other end seemed to have calmed down. Joe didn't hear the rest of the conversation clearly. Daisy said goodbye and ended the call.

"What I said earlier, about the hardest thing I've ever done?" she asked, and when he nodded, she continued. "I was wrong. Could we finish the tree and not discuss this?"

"I get it," he said. "I think the front tree should be silver and green."

"You're obviously color blind, so you don't

get to make choices," she said with a slight catch in her voice.

When they moved to the sitting room to decorate, she handed him a box of bulbs that he was allowed to use.

"You take this very seriously," he said.

"Very," she agreed with a twinkle in her silver-gray eyes.

He reached out and brushed hair back from her face, knowing that touching her would make him want to kiss her, but today wasn't a day for kissing. He was there for her, giving her someone to talk to, someone to count on. Someone who didn't take.

"Don't you have to go?" she asked.

He glanced at his watch. "I do. But I don't want to."

"I'm fine. Don't miss this time with your dad."

"When do you get the twins back?"

"Tomorrow. Cheryl called and she will bring them back to me. She wants to see how they act when she returns them. I'm not sure why."

"If you need me, will you please call me?"

She smiled. "I won't need to call. You always seem to show up just in time."

"What if I don't?"

She gave him a quick hug. "Don't ruin the moment and be too serious. Please."

"I won't."

"And you're not going to kiss me goodbye, are you?"

He shook his head. "No, I don't think I will. Today is about friendship. We've both got to figure out what we want and where we're going now that our pretend engagement has ended."

"Joe, there's nothing to figure out. I'll never marry again, and you deserve someone whole and full of faith. Isn't it the Proverbs 31 wife that men want?"

He didn't even know how to respond to that.

"I guess I need to go home and read Proverbs 31, so I know what it is I'm looking for."

With that he walked out.

Chapter Thirteen

The twins didn't come home Thursday morning. At noon she sat down with Leena to discuss safety protocol for Faith House, and also a plan should Leena's husband show up. They also discussed how safe it was to return to Holly's as a waitress.

When the phone rang, both women jumped. "Answer it," Leena encouraged.

Daisy reached for the cell phone on the table next to her. "Hello, this is Daisy."

"Daisy, this is Cheryl." A long pause. Daisy had known it was Cheryl. She didn't want small talk. She wanted to know why the twins hadn't arrived yet. Had they decided things went so well, they would just leave them with Lindsey?

"Good morning, Cheryl."

"Daisy, I'm sorry to say that things have not gone as planned," Cheryl said. "Lindsey and the twins are gone. We're not sure what happened. It appears they left sometime in the night."

"Oh no," Daisy whispered. There were several things she'd expected Cheryl to tell her. But not this.

"I'm sorry. This is not the call I wanted to make this morning. I was hoping to show up and find Lindsey and the twins having breakfast together. We're looking for them right now. I want to assure you, we're doing our best to find them."

"They could be anywhere," Daisy answered. "They might have left the state."

"Do you know anyone out of state she might have gone to?" Cheryl asked.

"I'm not sure. At one time she had a cousin in Illinois, maybe an uncle in Texas. She doesn't have a lot of family."

"I'll let you know as soon as I know something."

Daisy's heart shattered into a million pieces as she ended the call. Leena put an arm around Daisy as she buried her face in her hands and tried to make sense of this. How could it happen that in less than 24 hours the twins were gone?

"Daisy, what happened?" Leena asked in her soft voice.

"Lindsey took the girls. They're gone."

"We'll pray," Leena assured her.

"Pray?" Daisy shook her head at the idea.

"Is there anything else we can do?" Leena asked.

"Pray," Daisy said a second time. This time as a request. And Leena did pray. It was the sweetest, most touching prayer that Daisy thought she'd ever heard. But it was more than that, it was genuine and it felt like the kind of prayer that would move mountains.

"Thank you."

But the twins didn't come home that day.

The last place Daisy wanted to be on Friday was the church, wrapping gifts and helping to put together the community Christmas event. She didn't want to get out of bed. She didn't want to move. She wanted Myra and Miriam but they were still missing.

"Are you going to make it?" Leena asked as the three of them, Daisy, Leena and little Daphne, headed for the side door of the church.

"I want to go look for them. I'm not sure how much longer I can do nothing," she told her as they got out of the car at the church.

Leena grabbed Daisy's hand with her left, squeezing tight. "They'll be okay. I've been praying since yesterday. God is watching out for those little girls."

"Sometimes prayers don't get answered," she

said harshly, which wasn't fair to Leena. "I'm sorry."

"You have every right to be upset." Leena gave her hand another squeeze, then let go. "I know that sometimes it seems like God isn't there. He's somewhere out there, not interested in our lives. But Daisy, I look back and I can see His fingerprints all over my life. I might not have noticed He was there, holding on to me, but He was."

Daisy wiped a finger under her eyes to stop the tears that flowed. She couldn't go into the church crying.

"And here I thought I was the one helping you."

Leena bumped shoulders with her. "Is there a rule that says we can't help each other?"

Daisy's emotions had been chipped away for the past thirty-six hours. She felt raw from worry and anger. Becky Stanford had been the person she'd always turned to for support. But she'd passed away last year. Since then, Daisy had kept to herself. But lately she'd realized she needed a friend, someone to talk to, to share with. Someone like Leena, who didn't judge.

She had convinced herself she was meant to help Leena. Maybe God had sent Leena at just the right time, to help Daisy. She considered the idea that Leena was more than a temporary resident. She was part of God's plan for Faith House.

"Thank you." Daisy gave the other woman a quick hug.

They were at the door of the church. She drew in a deep breath and smiled at Daphne. The little girl with the pixie face, blond curls and big eyes smiled, revealing her deep dimples.

"Aren't you the cutest little peanut?" Daisy kissed the child's forehead.

Daphne wrapped thin arms around Daisy's waist. "I love you."

The little girl took hold of Daisy's hand. Together they opened the door and walked into the church.

Dixie greeted them in the hall, excitement overflowing because Daisy had arrived. The girl bounced around them like a Ping-Pong ball. She was exactly what Daisy needed.

"You finally showed up!" Dixie exclaimed as she grabbed first Leena in a hug and then Daisy.

"Did you think I wouldn't?" she asked.

Dixie pulled back. "Well, I know you don't care for church."

"I'm trying," she answered honestly.

"I know. I've been praying for you. I only thought you'd be further into my plans by now." Dixie, twelve-years-old and full of faith and wisdom—and energy.

Holly exited the room where the gifts were being kept, saw them and smiled before wagging a finger at Dixie. "Maybe it's supposed to be God's plan and not yours?" she asked.

Dixie shrugged off her mother's question. "I mean, I think God likes my plan. And I talked to Nana El about it and she's praying, too."

Ah, now it all made sense.

"God isn't a matchmaker," Daisy told the girl in a quiet voice. "And even if he was, I'm not interested."

She didn't need it spelled out for her. She knew what Dixie had been praying. Leena gave Daisy a sympathetic look as she walked to where the other women were waiting. As they entered the room filled with strangers, Daphne held tight to her mother. Daisy hoped, in time, the little girl would feel safe. For now, her mom was what she needed.

Joe had gotten an order of protection for Leena and Daphne. Her husband would be arrested if he got within 500 feet of her. As long as he understood that, they would all breathe a little easier.

Daisy knew too well that telling an abuser to maintain a distance didn't mean the abuser would obey the directive.

Dixie led Daisy farther into the room. Daisy surveyed what the churches and the community had managed to do. The room she'd stepped into was filled with toys, coats, winter boots and baskets of food. Next to her, Dixie grinned.

"Isn't it great?"

"It's amazing," Daisy agreed.

Dixie had glued herself to Leena and Daphne. "Allie and I are playing in the nursery. Do you want us to take Daphne?"

Leena looked to Daisy, unsure. "I think if she wants to go, that would be good."

"We have snacks," Allie, one year younger than Dixie, informed Leena. "Cookies and juice."

Leena handed her daughter over to Dixie. Not surprisingly, Daphne went to the girl. Leena looked a little lost without her daughter on her hip, but Rebecca quickly pulled her into a group that was tagging sizes on coats.

Daisy stood in the center of the room, lost again. No one knew about the twins. She hadn't shared. She should have, but how did she tell them? And if she did tell them, the mood in the room would shift. It would no longer be this joyous celebration.

Leena glanced her way, acting as if she meant to say something.

"How can I help?" Daisy asked. She stepped forward, making herself a part of the group.

"Tell us about the engagement," someone

asked. Someone who obviously didn't know that the entire thing had been a sham.

"I think you all should tell me how many people usually show up for this community Christmas?" Joe's Nana El came around a table at the far side of the room, her white hair framing her face and a spunky blue hat perched on top of her head. "I'm very impressed that you have such a large event."

"Our small town knows how to come together," Kylie responded. "We've done this for several years, and each year the event gets bigger, with more outreach and more gifts. It helps that all of the churches come together for the event."

"It's a wonderful program," Eloise assured her. "I'm very glad we were able to stay and help. We've enjoyed our time in your little town and in your church."

"Where are the twins?" Edith Collier asked. She'd been a Sunday-school teacher here when Daisy was little. She remembered her as a woman who always brought the best oatmeal cookies.

Thinking of those cookies didn't help at all because the moment the older woman mentioned the twins and gave her a soft sympathetic look, the tears flowed. Daisy brushed them away and put on a watery smile because that's what she did. She smiled through the pain. She made things better when they were really falling apart.

"They're with their mother for a visit," she lied.

Daisy took the roll of wrapping paper Holly held in her hand. She needed something to do, some way to get her mind off the pain that wouldn't go away.

"I'll wrap gifts," she told no one in particular. She needed to be busy.

Nana El touched her arm. "I'll wrap with Daisy," she announced, grabbing rolls of tape.

"That's great." Holly pointed them to a stack of presents and explained the labeling system.

"I'm sorry I'm such a busybody," Eloise said after wrapping several gifts and placing them on a cart to be taken to another room and sorted.

"You're not," Daisy told her.

Eloise laughed. "Oh, I am, I am. I'm a busybody who wants to see her family happy and settled. Joe is settled here in Hope. He had an inheritance, and he invested it wisely. But he isn't happy. Or he wasn't happy...until you."

"Nana El, you know that we're not really engaged."

Eloise gave her a questioning look. "Oh, I know that. But I also know something about the looks the two of you give one another."

"They're usually sarcastic, and sometimes accusing."

"Exactly. You're friends."

"Maybe," she admitted.

"Friendship is a good place to start." Eloise seemed determined.

Daisy was just as determined. "Nana El, I don't plan on getting married. Ever. I've been married and it isn't something I want to repeat."

"What part is it you don't want to repeat? The marriage or the abuse?"

Daisy blinked a few times, shocked by the direct question. Today wasn't the day to have this discussion; her emotions were too raw.

"I'm old, Daisy, I get to ask the hard questions that everyone else is afraid to ask." Eloise winked. "Don't look so stricken."

"I'm not, I just…" Daisy didn't know what to say.

"I won't push. If friendship is what you need right now, then I hope that you and Joe will be the best of friends." Then Eloise grew serious. "I hope the two of us will also be friends. Joe's father is buying a lake house, and I plan on spending more time here in Hope."

"I think we can definitely be friends," Daisy assured the other woman. She truly liked Nana El.

Daisy's phone buzzed, and she went cold as she looked at the caller ID.

"Are you okay?" Nana El touched her arm. "Do you need to take that?"

"I do," she agreed. "I'll be right back."

She stepped into the hallway but kept walking as she answered.

"Hello?"

"Daisy, it's me, Cheryl. Lindsey was stopped just outside of Oklahoma City. The twins were with her. They're okay."

The twins were okay. Relief washed over her. Tears rolled down her cheeks. She didn't fight the emotions. The past twenty-four hours had been too exhausting.

"Why would she do this?" Daisy asked as she went out the side door of the church.

She stood in the misty, cool weather, trying to come to terms with what Cheryl was telling her. Lindsey had tried to run off with the girls. This was the decision Lindsey had made. Why? When it would have been so easy to wait, knowing the girls would be coming back to her if she could maintain sobriety, stay clean, keep working.

"She isn't clean," Cheryl said in her no-nonsense way. "She's positive you're going to get permanent custody, and she thought that taking the kids to Mexico would ensure she could keep them. Unfortunately, she's done everything wrong. They've taken her and her boyfriend into custody, and they could possibly be charged not only for taking the girls but also for possession."

"So, what now? Where are they?"

"They're bringing them back to Tulsa."

"Can I come get them?"

Cheryl took a moment to answer. "Yes, you can. But we've got to discuss a permanency plan. At this point we're still looking at reunification but because of this stunt, the plan might change. Termination of parental rights is a big possibility."

Termination of parental rights. She knew the term, but that had never been the plan. Lindsey was a good person who wanted her girls back with her.

"She loves her girls. I really thought she would be able to do this for them."

Cheryl sighed. "Oh Daisy, of course she loves her daughters. But unfortunately, she is an addict. And she hasn't taken the necessary steps to get clean. Right now, the addiction is winning. What we need to discuss is what you want to do. If you're not interested in a permanent situation, raising the twins, then we should think about moving them to a home that is looking to adopt."

"I don't know." She looked up at the gray misty sky, aware that she was getting wet because she'd left her coat inside. "I love them, but I've constantly told myself they're Lindsey's girls. They're going home. That was the plan. Being their mom was never the goal."

She loved the twins. She'd been protecting her heart, telling herself that someday they would leave. They wouldn't always be hers.

The rain suddenly quit. At least it stopped raining on Daisy. A jacket settled over her shoulders. A jacket that smelled of the outdoors, hay, spicy cologne. Joe.

She glanced back, giving him a tight smile. He didn't smile. He stood behind her, protecting her, holding an umbrella over her head.

"They'll be here in less than two hours, Daisy. You don't have to make this decision right now. But we do have to start thinking toward permanency. I like you, but my goal is finding the best situation for the twins. If you aren't committed to raising them, we need to make a Plan B. I'll give you until after Christmas."

"Thank you, Cheryl. And I'll be there as soon as possible."

"Be safe."

Daisy ended the call with a soft "goodbye" and slipped the phone in her pocket.

Joe stood behind her; the umbrella he'd been holding remained over her head. She wanted to turn into his embrace because she needed his warmth and the solidness of his presence, but she couldn't face him.

"Are you okay?" he asked.

She drew in a breath because it was so Joe. It was deep, rumbling and safe. It made her wish she was anyone other than who she was, because she didn't know how to be the type of woman he would want.

She was scarred, broken and too independent.

Joe didn't know if he should ask her what had happened or walk away.

"Where are you going?" he finally asked.

"I have to go to Tulsa." She hesitated, standing in front of him, water dripping from her hair and sliding down her cheeks. She brushed the dampness away. "Thank you for the umbrella."

"You're welcome." He raised his right arm to push his hat back as he continued to hold the umbrella with his left. "I should just go. I'm not one to push my way in where I'm not wanted. But I can't seem to walk away."

"Because you think I need to be rescued?" she asked, her voice tremulous.

"I know you don't need to be rescued, Daisy. I know you're strong. I probably believe that about you more than you believe it yourself. I'm offering you friendship right now because you look as if you need a friend today."

"I could use a friend," she admitted. She swiped at the moisture dripping down her face, and he no longer believed it was rain.

"We should go inside out of the rain," he suggested as he guided them toward the church.

"I have to go," she told him as they neared the church.

"Maybe you could tell me what's going on?"

She closed her eyes briefly and nodded. She attempted to tell the story and more tears came. She swiped them away as his arms came around her, holding her tight.

"Whatever it is, I'm here."

"Lindsey left with the twins. The caseworker went to pick them up yesterday and they were gone."

Silence, his left hand firm on her back. "And you didn't tell anyone."

"Leena knew."

"That's a start. At least you let someone in." He stepped back. "As a friend, this hurts. I think you should know that. When people care about you, Daisy, it hurts when you shut them out of your life."

"I'm sorry."

"Maybe you should tell your family, too?" he suggested. "And then we can make a plan for leaving."

He was taking over. She stood on a precipice. One step forward and she'd let all of these people in her life. She wouldn't be able to hide anymore.

But wasn't that the reason for coming home?

Joe opened the front door of the church and waited. Daisy stood at the bottom of the steps looking up at him, and the look on her face told him she knew she had to make changes. He waited, wanting her to make the decision to let him in. When she joined him on the top step, he released his breath.

He took her hand and led her into the sanctuary where they could be alone. The warmth of the church greeted them. And the peace. The sanctuary was part of the original church. The pews were wood with cushions, the windows were stained glass, the woodwork was dark and showed years of polish and warmth.

When he entered this place, he felt God's presence. He didn't need a sermon or music, he needed only to be here and be still. To his way of thinking, people worried a lot about the right music, the length of service, the fiery messages, and they forgot to take time and be still in the presence of the Lord.

"Let's sit up here," he told her as they walked to the front of the church.

"Near the front and closer to God?" she quipped.

"I like to think so." He sat next to her, the folded umbrella on the floor in front of them. "Really, it doesn't matter where I sit, as long as I sit quietly and in His presence."

She remained close, leaning into him just a little. "I am sorry."

"I know you are. I hope you know, I'm here. I'm in, Daisy. I need for you to trust me."

"I don't know. I just…"

She didn't have to say it. He knew. She didn't trust. She thought she could carry it all on her own and not turn anything over to friends, family or God. It pained him to think that. It wounded his pride more than a little, but it tore a man-size chunk out of his heart.

"Let me help. I want to help." He didn't think he could make it any clearer.

"I don't want to burden you with all of my problems."

"I'm a big boy."

"I know you are. You're also a good and decent man. Someday you're going to find a woman who is as kind and decent as you are."

He laughed at that. He couldn't help himself. "Oh, right, my Proverbs 31 wife. Because I want someone perfect?"

What she didn't get was that he knew exactly what he wanted in a wife.

She gave him the stink eye for laughing. "It's all I've ever heard. A good, godly man wants his Proverbs 31 wife. She's virtuous, godly, hardworking, can raise decent children and she makes him look good by being diligent and industrious."

"I'm not looking for a Stepford wife. I'm looking for a flesh and blood human being."

She shook her head. "It doesn't matter. I need to get to Tulsa to pick up the twins."

"I'll drive you."

"I don't need to be driven."

"Close your eyes and hold out your hands," he ordered.

She gave him another narrow-eyed look, but she did as he told her. He caught her trembling hands in his left hand and held them. When she opened her eyes, he was caught off guard by the pain in those silver-gray depths.

"What was that about?" she asked.

"The only way to prove to you that you need someone to drive you. Your hands are shaking. You won't be able to focus on the road."

"So…"

"I'm your friend."

She closed her eyes and nodded. "Would you please drive me to Tulsa to get the twins? I'll have to make sure Leena is safe before I go. And I'll need to get car seats from my car."

"We should be going then."

They stood up and she studied him intently. "If I was a different person with a different past…"

He tried to laugh it off. "That's what all the girls say." But her words hurt him deep down. What would it take to get her to trust him with her heart?

Thirty minutes later they were on the road to Tulsa.

"What's going to happen now, with Lindsey?" he asked after she'd told him the details she'd gotten from the caseworker.

"I'm not really sure. I'm not sure what type of charges will be filed, if any. They might change the case plan to termination of parental rights instead of reunification." She started to sob and covered her face with her hands.

"I'm sorry, Daisy."

"I am, too. I wonder, did I do something to make her think running was the only option? I wanted to help her."

"I think she ran because she was desperate to keep her little girls but not desperate enough to make better choices."

"She's smart and talented. This shouldn't be her life."

"She made a choice. In that one moment, she made the wrong decision. We make choices about the food we'll eat, the road we take, the job we apply for and the friends we allow into our lives. And sometimes we make a choice to take a pill, or one more pill, or we take a chance that a drug is really going to give us the high our friends promise it will. And some of us don't come back from the one time. That one choice."

"I'm sorry for hurting you," she said quietly, her gaze on him as he drove. He glanced her way, gave her a quick smile and glued his attention back to the road in front of him.

"I'm fine. I learned my lesson," he managed to grin. "Next time a beautiful woman claims to be my fiancée, I might look a little more closely at the disclaimer."

"Beautiful woman, huh?" She sounded as though she was teasing, but she looked unsure.

"Very. But for now, I'll count myself fortunate that she'll hang with an ugly old dog like myself."

"Don't," she said.

He knew well enough to let it go.

"What will you do if they terminate Lindsey's parental rights?"

"I don't know. I'm a single woman. Don't they deserve a mom and dad, a real family? What can I give them?"

"A person who is committed to loving and caring for them."

"You make me sound really good." She smiled as she said it, and he wanted her to smile again.

"Almost Proverbs 31 good," he told her.

She laughed. "Let's not push it. I really don't know what to do. Cheryl said if I'm not interested in being their permanent guardian, they need to move them to a home that is, so they can get bonded with a family interested in adopting."

"I'm sorry."

"Me, too."

He almost proposed to her. For a guy not prone to impulsive behavior, that would have been over the top. A guy didn't propose to a woman he'd really only gotten to know recently. A man especially didn't propose to a woman who had scars she tried to hide and a determination to never again marry.

So instead of declaring his love for this woman, he kept on driving to Tulsa.

Chapter Fourteen

Daisy sat on the floor of Jack's living room, holding Miriam as Myra stood in front of her, clasping her hand. Across the room, Jack clapped his hands and called to the little girl.

"Myra, you big girl. Come to Papa Jack."

Daisy felt her heart do a little flip. Myra clapped her hands, mimicking Jack. She giggled and then took a step. "Pop," she said.

Jack laughed. "You call me anything you want!"

Myra clapped again, fell on her bottom, then pushed to her feet and took a second step. Maria got down on the floor and called to her.

"You come here, precious girl. Soon you will be walking all over, and Mama won't be able to keep up with you."

"I don't think they should call me Mama," Daisy said. "I don't know what's going to happen, and I don't want them to be confused. I went into this wanting to give them love and stability for as long as they needed me. But I think I have to know how to let them go, and make letting go easy for them."

"It's been a tough few days," Jack told her. "I think you need to take a step back and remember that God has a plan."

"Does he, Jack?" she asked. "Everyone keeps telling me that, and I keep trying to see it."

"Sometimes we don't see it until later. When we look back and realize, 'oh, that's what He was doing. He knew this was coming so He prepared me.' I think if you're honest, you could look back and see those moments."

Could she? One moment stuck out. The night Joe had rescued her. She hadn't thought about it in a long time, but the memories of that night had slowly drifted back in, reminding her she'd almost made one very bad choice. Where would she have ended up if Joe hadn't appeared that night and taken her home? What if Lindsey hadn't come to work for her and there hadn't been anyone to take the twins?

"Give it time," Jack said encouragingly. Then he pointed. "Look at her go."

It wasn't Myra doing the walking. Miriam had pushed to her feet and was taking tentative steps in the direction of the Christmas tree.

"We've got a walker!" The whispered exclamation came from the opening that led from the dining room into the living room. Kylie gave a little wave. "We came to visit."

Carson, Maggie and Adam appeared behind her. The four of them entered the living room, Maggie immediately went to the twins. Adam went to Maria and sat next to her, spinning the toy top that he liked to carry with him.

Carson, chose the chair next to where Daisy sat on the floor. "They seem to be bouncing back after their big adventure."

"They are. Myra said 'Pop' for 'Papa,' and look at Miriam go."

"Any news on their mother?" Carson asked.

She shook her head. "None that I know of. She's still in jail. They booked her for intent to distribute."

"That's a tough one. I know this isn't what you expected."

"No, it isn't."

Daisy had moved close to the tree, smiling when Carson's son moved to sit next to her, not speaking. Adam rarely spoke. He had changed and grown since Carson's marriage to Kylie, but he still rarely spoke, his autism seeming to keep him locked in his own world. But he did smile up at her and wink.

"I don't need anything else for Christmas,"

she announced when she hugged him. "That was the best gift ever."

"The best gift ever," Adam said in a rare moment of communication. He continued to play with the top. Spinning it over and over. He looked up at her with a sly smile. "Like Jesus."

She hugged him tight and he told her, "Nope."

She let go.

The twins abandoned their toys and crawled to her. Both stood, each with a hand on her shoulder. They touched the ornaments on the tree and she watched, stopping them when they pulled too hard.

Adam, not a fan of the twins, moved a short distance away.

"We should get a family photo," Jack suggested in a raspy voice.

"I'll take it," Maria offered. "Jack, you get over there with your children and grandchildren."

"And we'll take one of you and Jack too," Kylie said with a sly smile. "The two of you and the grandchildren."

"Yes, Maria, a picture of us." Jack squeezed her hand. "I think that in the spring, we'll have a wedding. Don't you agree?"

Maria's cheeks turned rosy. "Maybe."

A family photo of herself and the twins.

Daisy shook her head, unable to form a thought that made sense. "I don't know."

"You'll want this picture," Kylie assured her. "Whatever happens, you'll want this moment with the girls captured. It's their first Christmas, Daisy."

Myra grabbed her hand and smiled up at Daisy, her toothy little grin so happy and innocent.

"Mama," she said, giggling.

Daisy picked them both up. And then she sat with them cuddled on her lap in front of the tree. They kissed her cheeks and Kylie snapped a photo.

"Perfect," Kylie told her.

"All of you," Maria ordered. "Come on now, everyone to the tree. We can get more pictures on Christmas Day. Our first big family Christmas. We'll get that fancy camera of Kylie's and set the timer so that everyone is together in the picture." Maria motioned for them all to move to the tree. She helped Jack to stand and then kissed his cheek.

Maria and Jack clearly loved each other. They probably had for quite some time.

Watching them helped Daisy to avoid other thoughts. She didn't want to think of the family Christmas, less than a week away. At some point the celebrations would include Joe. She would have to come to terms with the fact that she would see him often, not just at Christmas. She had to accept that it would hurt for a time, but then it would get easier.

They all gathered around the tree. Daisy leaned in next to her dad. This would be the first time in twenty years that the two of them had been photographed together. She rested her hand on his shoulder, and the twins were settled on his lap.

"I'm so glad you're home," Jack told her as Maria snapped another picture.

"So am I." And she meant it. She'd come home for this, to find a way to repair her past because she'd known that she needed to have her family in her life.

She hadn't realized how much she needed Jack until that moment when he reached for her hand and gave it a light squeeze.

"I hope you'll forgive me," he said.

"I forgive you," she said, then kissed his cheek.

Her heart shifted as it began to mend.

"Do you want to help me with snacks?" Kylie asked after Maria had taken pictures. Too many pictures. The kids were starting to rebel. They wanted to play, not sit still. Even the twins were yelling "No, no, no."

"I'll watch the girls," Carson offered. "Go."

"I feel like the two of you have ulterior motives."

She went with Kylie anyway.

"What are we really doing?" she asked her sister-in-law as they left the room.

Kylie pointed to herself. "Do you doubt me?"

"I know when you have your therapist hat on, yes."

Kylie dug around in the cabinet and pulled out a popcorn maker. "I'm innocent. I mean, unless you want to talk. You do have a lot going on right now."

"No, not really. I mean, the situation with the girls but that's all." It was overwhelming, really. She hadn't slept since the day she'd taken them to Lindsey's place.

"It isn't about me," she told Kylie. "I love the twins. I don't want to give them up. But this isn't about what I want. It's about what is best for them. Am I the best thing for them? I'm not even sure if I can take care of myself, so how am I supposed to give them the best life. Don't they deserve two parents, maybe some siblings? You and Carson. You are the type of people who should raise little girls, not me."

"The fact that you care so much might be a good indicator that you're best the person to raise them. I'm not saying that Carson and I won't someday adopt. But these little girls,

Daisy, if they can't be with their biological mom, they should be with the woman who has been their mother. That woman is you. The state gave them to you and trusted you to care for them."

Daisy leaned against the counter and watched as Kylie started the popcorn. "I'm praying about it. And don't start jumping up and down, because I know you all have been praying for me and this is some sign that God has answered your prayers."

"I would never jump up and down," Kylie told her. "I might on the inside but never physically."

They both laughed.

"I'll be praying for you, too," Kylie told her. "Okay, that takes care of the twins. Now on to your fiancé."

"Former *fake* fiancé," Daisy corrected. "That was obviously not my best moment, but I've asked his parents to forgive me, and we've obviously ended the charade. Joe can go back to his regularly scheduled life, and I can go back to mine."

"Except that maybe the two of you like each other."

"Except that dating anyone isn't on my to-do list right now," Daisy explained. "I've been married before. I trusted a man who protected me, bought me flowers, took me on lovely dates, then tried to cut my throat."

"You think that there are no men who can be trusted, is that it?"

"There are men who can be trusted," Daisy said as she watched the popcorn grow inside the popcorn maker. "The problem is, how do you know the good ones from the bad ones?"

"Trust."

"Trusting has only ever gotten me hurt." She reached to unplug the popcorn maker because it was full to the top.

"I know you're afraid," Kylie said as she dumped the popcorn into a bowl. "I would be afraid, too. But what if you miss something amazing, something that was meant to be, all because you let your fear control you?"

"Thanks for making me feel like a coward," she teased.

What if she let fear keep her from doing what she was meant to do? What if she let the twins go and never saw them again? All because she was too afraid to be their mother.

What if Joe Lawson was meant to be hers and she missed out? What if she was too afraid to let him into her life?

It was silly to focus on those thoughts when the truth was, Joe hadn't called her since they returned from Tulsa. He'd made the trip with her and, as she'd known, he'd been her rock. But then he'd brought her home and left without a word. He didn't promise to call. He didn't offer to check in on them.

Kylie gave her a nudge, bringing her back to the present. "It's going to work out."

Daisy agreed. "I know it is."

Because being here with her family, in her childhood church, she honestly believed that no matter what, it would work out.

Joe had dinner with his family Saturday evening. It was his parents, Nana El and him. His sister, her husband and children would be coming in at the beginning of the week, then everything would change because there would be three children under the age of ten.

They were washing dishes at the sink, he and Nana El, when she tugged at his hair and gave him a scornful look.

"What was that for?" He pulled away in time to keep her from pinching his cheeks or something equally humiliating.

"You should get a trim," Nana El informed him.

"I don't need a trim," he answered.

"Women don't like their men shaggy and…" She waved her hand around.

"And what?" he asked. And he shouldn't have asked. That's what.

"Frumpy," she said.

"Frumpy?" He couldn't help but laugh. "Frumpy is the way you describe an older librarian with a navy dress with a white collar and heavy shoes."

"I guess if she was a librarian in 1949," his grandmother said.

"Either way, I'm not frumpy."

Grumpy maybe, but not frumpy.

"You're very sensitive," his grandmother said.

"Are you trying to make me feel bad?" he asked.

"She just wants you to make a good impression," his mother informed in her driest tone. Her smile gave away her amusement. "She'd hoped to be planning a Christmas wedding next year."

"I think you should probably count that one out," he said. "And I don't know why you were planning anything. You're the one person who guessed from the beginning that our engagement wasn't real."

"You might have worked it out." His grandmother patted his cheek. "It's because you're frumpy."

"You're making me grumpy," he told her. "And that rhymes with frumpy."

His mother and grandmother both laughed.

"Well, you could try a little harder," Nana El told him. "Wear something other than these plaid shirts and jeans. If you're going to wear boots, get some nice ones. Leave that cowboy hat at home. You're a Lawson."

"I'm a rancher now, Nana."

She arched a brow and nearly rolled her eyes at him. That move would have gotten him grounded twenty years ago. On his grandmother, it was cute.

"A rancher can still wear a suit from time to time, can't he?"

"I own a suit. Does that count?"

"It counts but only if you wear it. Maybe tomorrow evening. And you might try to be charming. Bring her roses."

He leaned to kiss her cheek. "Nana, I'm not sure what you want me to do, but in this, I am a Lawson. Lawsons are charming. But they also don't beg."

"Of course you aren't going to beg. You're going to charm. It'll come to you."

"What will?" Now he was confused.

"The part where you charm her," she said as if it all made perfect sense.

He looked to his mother for help. She lifted one shoulder in an elegant shrug. "I can't help you."

"Where's Dad? He could help me with this."

"He's looking at lake homes with fenced yards with the real estate agent. Because he wouldn't want the twins to fall into the lake."

"The twins," he said.

He didn't want to think about the twins, not while their future hung in the balance. He understood why Daisy didn't want to make an impulsive decision about their future. Adopting two little girls was huge. It was a lifetime commitment. It would change her entire life.

He wanted it to be their lives that it changed. Together. He wondered if that would make it different for her. If she knew she could trust him?

Only God knew the answer to that question.

Chapter Fifteen

"What are you doing?" Colt asked as Daisy sneaked out of the costume closet and headed for the fellowship hall.

"I'm on my way to watch Dixie in her play. She's a camel who doesn't want to follow the star."

"I know what she is. She's my daughter."

She made a face at him. "I know she's your daughter. I'm just saying, it's a perfect part for her and I don't want to miss it."

"Where are the twins?" Colt asked as he fell into step next to her.

"With Kylie and Carson." She told him.

"You are not going to ditch those little girls."

"Ditch them?"

"Because you think you can't be the mom, you're trying to find someone else to take them."

She raised a hand to stop him. "I think you

should stop right there, mister, because living in your glass house, you can't throw stones at mine. Especially when you haven't bothered to have a conversation with me about this situation."

"I'm sorry," he apologized. Then he leaned in and whispered to her, "We're having a baby."

"What? Oh!" She hugged him tight. "Then I forgive you."

"For everything?" he joked, pulling back, clearly astounded.

"You never really did anything to me."

"I wasn't there to help you, protect you." He studied her. "Are you okay?"

"Yeah, I am." She was learning to trust. And to trust, she realized, she had to give up pieces of herself, accepting that sometimes people might let her down. But most of the time they wouldn't.

But she couldn't punish all of the people in her life for the past mistakes of a few. And she couldn't punish a good man for the sins of a man who had hurt her.

"We need to go. We can't miss the play." She took Colt by the hand and led him back to the fellowship hall. The tables were filled with families, friends, strangers getting to know one another. The stage in the corner had become a starry night in the desert. The camels, led by the

Magi, were traveling to Bethlehem, which happened to be a small corner of the stage where Mary, Joseph and baby Jesus waited.

"Do these guys have any idea where we're going?" one camel asked the other.

"They're men," said Camel Two, which happened to be Dixie. "They never ask for directions."

"Not true," said Camel Three. "They asked that king guy. Remember the one who told us to come back and fill him in on all of the details. I had a bad feeling about that guy."

"Did you see the star?" asked Camel One. "I know we don't have a GPS, but I heard a story once about a star and something about the city of David. Isn't that the city, right there ahead?"

Camel Two snorted. "I think we're going in circles. I really think they don't know where we're going. Did they even read the directions?"

Everyone laughed.

"I have to go," Daisy told her brother.

"Where are you going?" Colt asked.

"Stay here and finish watching the play. Your kid is fantastic."

Colt looked worried. "Daisy?"

"I'm fine. Don't worry, this is something I have to do."

"It isn't anything crazy?"

"It's kind of crazy," she assured him. "But what would you expect from me?"

"I expect you to be brave and do something that makes you happy."

"That's what I'm doing," she assured him.

Joe watched the play from the side of the fellowship hall. He laughed at the camels, feeling something stir deep within as the Magi found the baby Jesus. The journey. The savior. It was somehow symbolic of each of their lives. Everyone took a journey, seeking something real, something that proved to be the foundation of their faith.

He ignored, with difficulty, Daisy as she stood off to the side with Colt. She never looked his way. Not once. Not that he'd expected her to.

The fact that he'd proven time and again that she could trust him and she'd rejected those actions wounded him. He wanted her to trust him, and not hold him accountable for the deeds of another person.

But he was working on letting it go. That's what God would have him do. He had to leave her to God, to work on her heart, to help her deal with her past. All he could do was take care of himself.

He studied the people in the fellowship hall, loving the reactions on their faces as they watched the play. There were families, singles, older folks, you name it, they all came. They laughed together, talked together and encouraged one another. This play and dinner made Christmas special for so many people. For Joe, it changed the entire holiday season.

This made it all real.

The play ended. People clapped and shouted. Joe joined the other men of his quartet, and they walked up on stage to sing the song they'd been practicing for several months.

As he took to the stage, he watched his grandmother wend her way through the crowd and then land with another group of ladies close to her age. They were a wild group, and they owned a small, older hotel on the lake. Silver Circle, they called it. Yes, his grandmother had definitely made herself at home in Hope.

The men started to sing. Joe had to jerk himself back to the task at hand, the music. His mind kept drifting. Staying focused became even more difficult when he spotted Isaac at a back door taunting him with a Santa costume. He shook his head at Isaac, who merely nodded as if Joe playing Santa was a done deal.

He knew he would end up wearing that suit but didn't want to give in too easily. He didn't like to let Isaac win.

"Ring the bell, ring the bell," he sang, almost

forgetting his place in the song and his lines. He turned his attention away from Isaac and spotted a bigger distraction. Kylie was passing the twins to Holly and Carson. She and Daisy were heading for the stage.

The song ended. He and the guys walked off the stage with people clapping and congratulating them on a job well done.

Kylie and Daisy took the stage. They waited for Mrs. Pillar to start the intro, and then they sang "Silent Night," just as they'd practiced a couple of weeks earlier.

The crowd had stopped talking. Everyone listened. Joe felt almost dazed by the performance. After the song was over, she and Kylie rushed off the stage. Kylie went back to sit with Carson; Daisy rushed out of the room.

Joe wasn't going after her. He had too much pride to beg her to give him a shot.

"What are you doing standing here like you don't have anything better to do?" Isaac came up beside him. "We have to get Santa to the sleigh."

"You go be Santa," Joe told his friend.

"I'm not as tall," Isaac told him.

"Santa isn't tall, he's round. Have you never read the story?" Joe started in the other direction. Isaac jumped in front of him.

Isaac pushed the suit, now in a box to hide it

from children, at Joe. "Please. All the kids are counting on this."

"Fine, but you're going to owe me big time. I'll meet you back on the stage."

"Thanks, Joe. You're the best."

Isaac tipped his hat as he grinned and walked away.

Joe hurried through the building because he wasn't going to let the children down. Isaac had counted on that, and he'd been correct. No way would Joe let the kids line up and not have a Santa.

He found an empty classroom to use as a dressing room. From the looks of it—posters on the walls, old sofas and bean bag chairs— he guessed it to be a youth room.

It did take him longer than expected to put on the suit, the beard, the wig. He looked in the mirror at the finished product. It wasn't good. Not good at all. The pants were too short. He'd had to put on his own cowboy boots because the Santa black boots were two sizes too small.

Before leaving the room, he grabbed a pillow off the sofa and shoved it under his shirt. A little padding might help him have more of a jolly St. Nick look.

He made his way back to the fellowship hall, where he was greeted by cheers and laughter.

He waved his gloved hand, then hurried to tighten the belt. Isaac met him, dressed as an elf.

"You're an elf." Joe shook his head. "I've been planning ways to get back at you for this costume, and you're wearing a pointy hat and pointy shoes."

Isaac grinned and tugged on his fake beard. "I thought you might approve. At least I'm not wearing my cowboy boots with a Santa suit."

"No way could I fit in the Santa boots. Next year, if I do this next year, I need a better wardrobe."

Isaac saluted. "No problem. Go ahead and have a seat. We have to get gifts ready, and Santa's helpers are getting it all together so we can move quickly. The kids will come up, but we'll already have their names and ages. The helpers will hand you the gift that matches the child."

"What do you do?" Joe asked his elf friend.

"I help kids through the line and keep them happy."

"Is that your chair?" Joe asked as he stepped on stage.

"What chair?" Isaac asked.

"The one next to mine?"

Isaac tugged at the beard again. "Not sure that's supposed to be there. You have a seat, and I'll see what we can do."

Joe sat down because what else could he do?

He practiced his "ho, ho, ho" a few times. It sounded pretty lame. And then someone sat down next to him.

"I have a gift for you," that someone said.

He turned sideways as Mrs. Claus handed him a gift.

"What's this?" he asked.

Daisy was the prettiest Mrs. Claus ever. She smiled at him. "I'm not sure you'll want it. It's kind of damaged, broken, a few other issues."

"Can I return it if I don't like it?"

"I wish you wouldn't."

"What is it?" he asked.

She leaned close.

"It's my heart."

His own heart tumbled all over itself when she said those words.

"But I didn't get you anything," he said.

"But you did. You've given me everything. Just promise that you'll take good care of my heart. It comes with another special gift."

"What's that?" he asked.

"Trust." Daisy's voice trembled on the word. "I give you my trust. It isn't easy for me, but there is no one I'd rather give it to."

"We can't do this here," he said. He waved Isaac the Elf to his side.

"What's up?" Isaac looked from Daisy to Joe. "Problems?"

"Santa is taking a quick break. Mrs. Claus and I need to talk."

"And kiss?" Isaac asked.

"And kiss."

"We're going to upset the children," Daisy warned Joe as he led her down the hall to an empty classroom.

"You can't show up with your heart and your trust and think I could just ignore that." He pulled her close and she stepped into his embrace.

"Kiss me Joe."

He kissed her. She locked her arms around his neck and he kissed her again, because he couldn't believe she was in his arms and it was real.

"What are you doing?" he asked after a minute.

"Learning to trust," she told him. "I'm learning to make mistakes and survive. I'm learning to trust and not make you pay for someone else's sin."

He held her and she stayed, happily so, in his arms. She smiled into his shoulder, knowing she'd taken him by surprise.

"What are we going to do?" he asked.

"We're going to date."

"Okay," he said.

"Because I think I love you. And I hope you love me back."

"I think that's a given," he told her, still holding her tenderly.

"I'm afraid you'll figure out how broken I am and realize that you never should have stepped a single—" she looked down at his feet "—boot into my life."

"I have already stepped into your life," he told her. "My only regret will be if you ask me to leave your life."

"I think I want to adopt the twins. I'm praying about that, and I think we should pray about it together."

"I'll pray," he promised.

She cupped his cheeks in her hands. "Then I hope you'll keep your gift. Don't regift it, please."

"Never. It's mine. It's perfect for me."

He kissed her again, then Isaac was there, telling them they had thirty seconds before small people would start a riot, demanding their gifts.

Daisy pulled back and they both laughed, she and her cowboy. She prayed that this day was just the beginning for them and that they would always find a way to laugh.

Epilogue

They walked into a courtroom on a beautiful day in September. The sky was clear blue, the air had turned a little cooler than the nearly 100 degrees of the week before. Daisy wore a pretty floral dress, and she'd allowed Rebecca to do her hair. It was a twisty, updo, with loose tendrils around her face. Soft and feminine, that's how Rebecca had described it. For today, soft and feminine seemed to be just the thing.

She'd left her scarf at home. She still wore it in public but more and more she found herself forgetting it.

She carried Miriam. Joe carried Myra.

She smiled at her handsome mountain of a cowboy. His grandmother, Nana El, was very pleased. He'd worn a suit. She had declared him the most handsome and charming Lawson of them all.

Daisy was inclined to agree.

Nana El and Joe Senior both took a seat. Joe's sister, Diana and her husband, Aiden, were sitting behind them.

Daisy's family crowded the other side of the courtroom. By family, she meant half the town of Hope, including Leena and Daphne. In the months since Christmas, Leena had become a good friend but she'd also stayed on at Faith House to help out. There had been several women coming through the house. Between Daisy and Leena, they'd managed to find them jobs, new homes and even helped a couple of women get job training and start college.

Joe, Daisy and the twins took a seat at one of the tables in front of the judge. Lindsey was not present. She'd signed herself into a rehab center, and then she'd asked to sign the paperwork to terminate her parental rights. They'd met with her the previous week. She'd held the twins and promised to continue to fight so that someday she could be in their lives. A promise that Joe and Daisy supported.

"This is an unusual proceeding," the judge began. "One of my favorite parts of my job. Today I get the honor of making families. And this family, all of you, are a part of that process. Today Joe and Daisy will become the parents of Myra and Miriam, from this day forward to be called by the last name of Lawson.

"Before we begin that proceeding, I've been asked to do another great honor. I'm going to perform the wedding ceremony for their parents to become Mr. and Mrs. Joe Lawson.

"Joe, if you'd like to come forward and stand before my bench. Daisy, your father has requested that you not join Joe at the bench. He'd like to walk you down the aisle. Joe, you have family and friends present. They'd like to stand with you."

Joe nodded, very nearly speechless for the first time in his life. He blinked away the tears as his parents, sister and brother-in-law and Nana El all came to the front of the courtroom to stand next to him. And then Isaac stood, leaving the other Wests, and joined Joe and family.

"I think I'm the best man." Isaac spoke in an oddly gruff voice as he swiped at his eyes.

"I'm honored to have you next to me," Joe told him.

He watched as Daisy and Jack stepped out of the courtroom. This was it, the moment he had waited for and prayed for. Daisy West would soon be Daisy Lawson. They would have two beautiful little girls, Myra and Miriam. And maybe someday, God willing, more children to fill the home he was building for them. He closed his eyes and said a silent, "Thank you," to God for answered prayers.

Outside the courtroom, Kylie was waiting with Holly and Rebecca. They handed Daisy a bouquet of fall flowers. The twins were with them in pretty floral dresses, similar to Daisy's. Dixie and Allie were there as well.

Jack opened the door of the courtroom. "Are you all ready?"

Daisy looked back at her sisters-in-law. "I'm ready."

The bridesmaids went first. The twins, with Allie and Dixie, followed closely behind.

"I plan on walking you down the aisle," Jack informed her. "I'm going to need help."

Maria joined them. She took Jack's right hand. Daisy tucked her left hand in his arm. The wedding march began to play. Daisy couldn't stop the tears that slid down her cheeks as she took slow and steady steps through the courtroom toward her future.

At the front, standing before the judge who was about to make them man and wife, and then parents, Joe stood with their daughters. She'd been so afraid of giving her heart to anyone, but this man had proven that he could not only take care of her heart, he could be a father to Myra and Miriam.

He was her present and her future. Together

they would become Mr. and Mrs. Joe Lawson. Together they would become parents. This day would always be known as the day they became one family.

* * * * *

If you loved this story,
pick up the other books
in the Mercy Ranch *series,*

Reunited with the Rancher
The Rancher's Christmas Match
Her Oklahoma Rancher
"His Christmas Family"
in Western Christmas Wishes
The Rancher's Holiday Hope
The Prodigal Cowboy

from bestselling author
Brenda Minton

Available now from Love Inspired!

Find more great reads at
www.LoveInspired.com

Dear Reader,

Thank you for visiting Mercy Ranch. The community of Hope, Oklahoma, and the residents of Mercy Ranch have become a second home to me and I hope you've enjoyed this journey as much as I have.

In this book you'll find the conclusion of the saga of Mercy Ranch and the West family. It seems only fitting that Daisy West has come home to make amends with her estranged father, Jack West, the owner of Mercy Ranch. Somehow along the way, she'll find love as well.

In her story you will find a story of trust, forgiveness and even contentment. I hope you enjoy this book and stay tuned for whatever comes next!

Brenda Minton

COMING NEXT MONTH FROM
Love Inspired
Available December 1, 2020

AN AMISH HOLIDAY COURTSHIP
by Emma Miller

Ready to find a husband at Christmastime, Ginger Stutzman has her sights set on the handsome new Amish bachelor in town. But she can't help but feel drawn to her boss, Eli Kutz, and his four children. Could the widower be her true perfect match?

A PRECIOUS CHRISTMAS GIFT
Redemption's Amish Legacies • by Patricia Johns

Determined to find a loving Amish family for her unborn child, Eve Shrock's convinced Noah Wiebe's brother and sister-in-law are a great fit. But when she starts falling for Noah, the best place for her baby might just be in her arms...with Noah at her side.

HIS HOLIDAY PRAYER
Hearts of Oklahoma • by Tina Radcliffe

Beginning a new job after the holidays is the change widower Tucker Rainbolt's been praying for. Before he and his twin girls can move, he must ensure his vet clinic partner, Jena Harper, can take over—and stay afloat. But could giving his heart to Jena be the fresh start he *really* needs?

CHRISTMAS IN A SNOWSTORM
The Calhoun Cowboys • by Lois Richer

Returning home to his Montana family ranch, journalist Sam Calhoun volunteers to run the local Christmas festival. But as he works with single mom Joy Grainger on the project, the last thing he expects is for her children to set their sights on making him their new dad...

THE TEXAN'S UNEXPECTED HOLIDAY
Cowboys of Diamondback Ranch • by Jolene Navarro

Driven to get her sister and baby niece out of a dangerous situation, Lexy Zapata takes a job near Damian De La Rosa's family's ranch and brings them with her. Now they can stay hidden through Christmas, and Lexy will start planning their next move...if she can ignore the way Damian pulls at her heart.

A DAUGHTER FOR CHRISTMAS
Triple Creek Cowboys • by Stephanie Dees

Moving into a cottage on Triple Creek Ranch to help her little girl, Alice, overcome a traumatic experience, single mom Eve Fallon doesn't count on rescuing grumpy rancher Tanner Cole as he struggles to plan a party for foster kids. Can she revive both Tanner's and Alice's Christmas spirit?
